Praise for *The Sadness of Beautiful Things*

"With a deceitful simplicity and a generously empathetic ear, Simon Van Booy gets to the core of the moment."
—Colum McCann, author of *TransAtlantic* and *Let the Great World Spin*

"Simon Van Booy writes wonderful stories that surprise and uplift, that hold our attention all the way with subtle revelations about life in all its astounding contradictions, its sorrows and joys."
—Sheila Kohler, author of *Becoming Jane Eyre* and *Once We Were Sisters*

Praise for Simon Van Booy's work

"Breathtaking . . . chillingly beautiful, like postcards from Eden . . . Van Booy's stories are somehow like paintings the characters walk out of, and keep walking."
—*Los Angeles Times*

"Simon Van Booy knows a great deal about the complex longings of the human heart."
—Robert Olen Butler, Pulitzer Prize–winning author of *A Good Scent from a Strange Mountain*

"Each of Van Booy's stories is moments of sheer loveliness."
—*Publishers Weekly*

PENGUIN BOOKS

THE SADNESS OF BEAUTIFUL THINGS

Simon Van Booy is the award-winning and best-selling author of nine books of fiction and three anthologies of philosophy. He has written for the *New York Times*, the *Financial Times*, the *Irish Times*, NPR, and the BBC. His books have been translated into many languages. He lives in New York with his wife and daughter. In 2013, he founded Writers for Children, a project that helps young people build confidence in their storytelling abilities.

The Sadness *of* Beautiful Things

Stories

∞

Simon Van Booy

PENGUIN BOOKS

PENGUIN BOOKS
An imprint of Penguin Random House LLC
375 Hudson Street
New York, New York 10014
penguinrandomhouse.com

LIBRARY OF CONGRESS CATALOGING-IN-PUBLICATION DATA
Names: Van Booy, Simon, author.
Title: The sadness of beautiful things : stories / Simon Van Booy.
Description: New York, New York : Penguin Books, [2018]
Identifiers: LCCN 2018018374 (print) | LCCN 2018019579 (ebook) |
ISBN 9780525504863 (ebook) | ISBN 9780143133049 (paperback)
Subjects: | BISAC: FICTION / Short Stories (single author). |
FICTION / Literary. | FICTION / Historical.
Classification: LCC PR6122.A36 (ebook) | LCC PR6122.A36 A6 2018
(print) | DDC 823/.92—dc23
LC record available at https://lccn.loc.gov/2018018374

Printed in the United States of America
1 3 5 7 9 10 8 6 4 2

Set in Berling LT Std   Designed by Elke Sigal

For S.D.S.
1968–2017

Contents

Acknowledgments

The author wishes to thank his publisher and editor, Patrick Nolan; editorial assistant, Matthew Klise; literary agent and friend, Carrie Kania.

A Sacrifice was first published in the *Irish Times*. A version of the *The Green Blanket* was first published in the Chinese edition of *ELLE*. *The Hitchhiker* was commissioned and broadcast by the BBC. A version of *The Doorman* was commissioned by the Chinese edition of *Harper's Bazaar*.

Preface

Most of the tales in this collection
are based on true stories told to me
over the course of my travels.

—*Simon*.

The Sadness
of Beautiful Things

He who binds to himself a joy
Does the wingèd life destroy;
But he who kisses the joy as it flies
Lives in eternity's sunrise.

—WILLIAM BLAKE

A Sacrifice

Until the fire, nobody much cared for the McCrutchens. They just weren't used to living in a town. The children were rowdy and unkempt and walked five abreast along the pavement, laughing at the old, and shouting silly things at other people's children.

Mr. and Mrs. McCrutchen had been married since they were teenagers. The service took place in a stone church. Maggie was a young bride, even by country standards. Standing barefoot in white, she concentrated on what the priest was saying, without truly understanding.

The groom's mother gave her a piece of silver jewelry and she wore it around her neck. The groom arrived with his friends. He wore a gold hoop in one ear. The sleeves of a dark suit fell over his knuckles.

They rode away on a chestnut horse.

To be a McCrutchen child meant knowing every detail of the story.

"It's just a matter o' time . . ." their mother would sometimes say when she put them to bed, "before the lot o' you start falling in love, one by one, like bottles knocked off a wall."

They moved to the village of Douglas because the school was known for being good. Mr. and Mrs. McCrutchen dreamed their children might get on in life. But then their house burned down.

Some said it was a cigarette or an unattended toaster. Others believed it was a candle blown into net curtains by wind.

There had not been a fire like this in Douglas for thirty years. The street had to be blocked off with orange cones. The neighbors were told to move their cars and stay far back. The McCrutchens bunched together on the glistening tarmac in their nightclothes. Firemen rushed about with hoses and ladders, trying to save the other houses.

Maggie McCrutchen was crying in front of everybody. The money her husband had given her to get insurance a year before, she had paid to the dentist. Her daughter had crooked teeth and people at school were laughing.

The children stayed with different neighbors, as no one had room for all seven. The next morning their blackened, dripping things were carried into the street. The Guards put up fences to keep people out. The youngest had left her doll in the panic to escape, so one of the fire inspectors came back after his shift to look for it, but had a new one in his pocket, just in case.

Then a month after the fire, very early, a fleet of workmen's trucks drove slowly up the street, then parked outside the charred ruin. The fences came down, and there were workers from Cork, and engineers from Dublin, tramping about in their boots with charts and cameras and special equipment that was yellow and orange.

The McCrutchens were living in a bungalow owned by the Church, near the quarry—a place empty for years and riddled with damp. But it cost nothing more than regular appearance at Mass.

When the McCrutchen children heard at school about the workmen and the ladders going up—they thought it was a joke. Eventually, a woman from the building department showed up at the bungalow. Signatures were needed so work could proceed.

At first everyone thought the Church had called in a favor from Rome, the Pope himself. But one of the workmen on his tea break said it was a neighbor who'd arranged everything through Dublin lawyers as they wished to remain anonymous. All the McCrutchens had to do was pick the tiles, choose the paint, and find carpet with a pattern they liked.

Dogs who'd barely left the hearth in years were now being dragged around the block several times a day. The hunger for gossip was insatiable. A few neighbors pretended they knew who it was but had been sworn to secrecy. Husbands coming home late from the pub on Friday night woke their wives to confess secret hoardes of euros.

Eventually someone on the street did find out. A woman called Penny Carr, known for her chrysanthemums.

This is how it happened.

About twelve months after the fire, the McCrutchens moved into their rebuilt home. They had a party and invited the neighbors, the Guards, the fire crew, the priest—and even some of the workers. Everyone had to take their shoes off, and the youngest McCrutchen children were charged with arranging them in size order by the front door.

There was a rumor the identity of the benefactor would be revealed at the party, and so the whole street packed the McCrutchen house, with drinking, eating, singing, dogs, and children running over the new carpet in their bare feet.

The only person not in attendance was Kitty O'Donnell, who lived at number seventy-seven. She had gotten fairly ill and most of the time was propped up in bed with the television on and something hot to drink.

Kitty was a local woman who'd grown up in the city of Cork nearby, then moved to Douglas with her husband when they got married. After he died she was alone.

The day after the McCrutchens' housewarming, Penny took some cake to her elderly neighbor. They had a nice talk. Mostly things on the news and the weather. The old woman kept patting Penny's hand.

"Do you not have many visitors, Mrs. O'Donnell?"

"Not so much. It's just me left now."

With her husband at work in the day, and their one daughter at college in Dublin, Penny decided to go over again a few days later. She called first on the telephone. Kitty said to use a key under the flowerpot.

The front room was full of still, gray light that seeped through delicate curtains of lace, now yellow with age. Mrs. O'Donnell said they had been from the time of her wedding. There were photographs of her husband in pretty frames, looking as Kitty remembered him from their long and happy life together. And it *had* been a good life. Better than most. Kitty knew that and was grateful for it.

The visits from her neighbor became regular. One day Kitty sat up too quickly and knocked over her tea. The mug didn't break, but the carpet was wet. Penny got down and soaked as much as she could into a hand towel.

"It was me, you know . . ." Mrs. O'Donnell said as her neighbor pushed on the stain, "what paid for the McCrutchens' house."

Penny laughed. "You, Kitty?"

"Aye."

"I never would have guessed it was you."

"Well, now you know."

"You're the secret millionaire on the street?"

"That's right."

Penny looked up, wondering if the old woman's mind was starting to falter. "Where do you keep it then? Under the mattress?"

"Down in the town, locked up in a bank for safekeeping."

When Penny thought the stain was faint enough she stopped rubbing and put the towel on the tray to go downstairs.

"I'm not joking, Penny. Do you promise to keep it under your hat?"

"Well, if you're the secret millionaire, Kitty—at least tell me how you came to have such a fortune. Lottery, was it?"

"You really want to know?"

"Aye."

"Because it's a long story and a sad one, so."

"I'm all ears, Kitty."

"Maybe on your next visit."

Penny laughed with some awkwardness. "If you want I can make some lunch and you can tell me after we've eaten?"

Mrs. O'Donnell couldn't resist. "You afraid I'll die before you come round again?"

Her neighbor's cheeks burned.

"I'll be ninety-two in the spring, Penny."

"I know, that's a grand age, so it is."

After opening a can of soup, then pouring it into a silver pot to heat, Penny looked around at all Kitty's things, searching for some clue to her wealth. But the interior of number seventy-seven was like every other home on the street. A sturdy kitchen table. Bills stacked behind a small, battery-operated clock. A bread bin full of little, hard crumbs. A cold fireplace in the sitting room, and a cabinet of ceramic figures painted in old clothes that were supposed to have value.

After eating the soup and brewing another pot of tea, Mrs. O'Donnell said she was ready. The story began in 1901. A little girl had just been born on a farm outside Douglas. Her name was Celia Riley. She had a nice time growing up, wandering the fields, walking her father to the pub, fetching water in buckets, the smell of green grass in summer, hay in winter. She was fifteen years old when she met someone. A boy, just a little older than herself, from a village in the north of Ireland. He was down helping in the fields, earning money in the warm weather.

After glancing at each other a few times, Celia and the

young man took walks. They weren't supposed to be alone, but could always find a quiet path outside the village. At the end of the summer the boy went with his brother to fight in France against the Kaiser. They both died in the first week. Why they went, nobody really knew. It might have been the adventure. Or an excuse to see Paris and hear a foreign tongue.

At first Celia thought it was sickness in her body from the shock of his violent death. She stayed in bed for several days being looked after by her mother.

Later on, it was clear to her what was happening. She sat her parents down in the kitchen and told them everything, the walks, the soft words, his promises, the brutal but honorable way he died—and lastly that inside her body was all that remained of him in the world.

Her mother studied the floorboards without moving. Then her father stood in his clean, heavy boots and went to the cupboard. The key was in his waistcoat pocket. Celia thought she was going to be given some money. But he took down his shotgun. Celia's mother rushed over and put her hands on it, but his mind was made up.

She was allowed to go upstairs and pack a few of her things. It was hard to see through such wet eyes.

He waited for her downstairs with the front door wide open, the gun over his arm, the twin barrels like hard, eyeless sockets. She could hear her mother's voice. A long, low petitioning whisper, then nothing.

Celia's father walked her to the edge of the village. People who were out stopped to look.

. . .

After he had gone back, she sat by the roadside and looked at things without really seeing them. Then her mother came. She sat with her and they held one another. Then they walked the long road into Cork. There was a convent with spiked gates that accepted girls in her situation. After a week, it was all arranged. Celia would carry the child. Then once it was born she would hand it over. The sisters already knew who the parents would be.

Celia could live at the convent and work for the nuns, but over the years, her mother had saved money from the odd scrap of sewing, and it was used for a ticket to America. There she could forget her mistake.

Eight months later, Celia gave birth to a girl. She had worked at the convent all that time and learned to hide inside the person everyone saw and spoke to.

During delivery, she was allowed to look at the baby, but not hold it, nor touch its face.

She was lucky, the sister said. Most girls had to stay in the convent and work for the Church the rest of their lives to atone for their sin against Him.

The voyage seemed to take a very long time. Celia met some nice people on the ship, who gave her advice about what to do when she got to America—what to say to the immigration men, and how to behave.

Her mother had arranged for work as a maid in a big house in lower Manhattan. She could receive letters from home, but could not send them.

It was hard work, but there was lots to eat in the evenings when the family went out and Celia could pretend it was her house.

After a few months, an earring went missing. Celia looked everywhere. The woman said that stealing was like lying to God. Celia didn't realize she was being accused, and agreed that it was a terrible sin to steal.

By that time, though, she had made a few friends. One of them lived in a house for girls run by a former schoolteacher, who agreed to give Celia a week or two of lodging until she could find a new situation.

But without a reference it was not easy. Celia imagined her former mistress discovering the earring, perhaps in the bedding. Then begging her to come back.

One day she noticed a sign in the window of a restaurant. It was where the Italian section began, but in the evenings, Celia liked to walk all over.

Help was wanted making dough. The restaurant was dark, with burgundy drapes and oil paintings of ruined castles and shipwrecks. It was outside regular eating hours, but in the kitchen, men were sitting on crates playing cards. When she told them she wanted to help make the dough, they took cigarettes out of their mouths and laughed. But one of them—a stocky Sicilian called Reggie—got up and asked what experience she had. Celia told them how, as a girl, she had made the family bread with her mother and knew all the tricks. When he spoke the other men were quiet. He had very dark skin and a barrel chest.

After a few months, she had learned a few words of Italian, and Reggie knew a folk song in Irish. As he was several inches shorter than Celia, they drew glances as he walked her back to the boardinghouse every night. Then he waited by the gate until the door had opened and she was inside.

A year later Reggie had saved and borrowed enough to open his own place. Would Celia work for him? She could be in charge, he said. Wasn't that what she wanted?

All this time Celia had been trying to keep away from her feelings, but she left her job to work with the ambitious Sicilian. He was right—she wanted to be in charge.

After another year, on one of their walks home, Reggie asked Celia to marry him. She quickly told him she couldn't, but when they got to her boardinghouse he waited at the gate like always, to make sure she got safely inside. And because of this, she accepted his proposal the next day.

Three years later they had four restaurants with a factory in the Bronx making pasta to supply other eating houses in the city. They were best friends as much as husband and wife—and while she knew about his temper, Reggie had never once raised his voice or spoken harshly in her presence.

Eventually, of course, she told him.

She had to.

It was too hard, she said, living out a marriage with a lie underneath. She feared her husband would be upset, and he was upset, but not for the reason she thought. He stood with his hands flat on the walnut desk.

"You gotta go back to Eyeland and get her."

"And bring her here, Reggie? To be with us?"

"That's right, but don't be surprised if she's taller than me."

"But what will people think? What will they say when I return with a child?"

"To hell with people."

"Will you come with me?"

He said that he would not. That it was something she needed to do alone.

A few days later, Celia Fidanzati sailed first-class on the *Blue Stork*. For most of the trip she stood on deck in her long coat. But sometimes she went down to the shared quarters and made friends with girls who were alone.

It was a week before Kitty O'Donnell's eighty-second birthday when a lawyer came from Dublin to see her. He was a partner at the law firm, and from his briefcase he took a folder with copies of Celia's marriage and death certificates stamped by the New York authorities. He also had photocopies of a newspaper article. Something from the obituary section of the *New York Times*. At the bottom of the article was a photograph of Celia and Reggie when they were first married—when the company was just the two of them.

Also in the lawyer's possession was a letter, written by Celia, that he offered to read aloud because Mrs. O'Donnell's hands were shaking.

The things written in the letter were difficult to accept.

The lawyer sat there and let her take it in. When she cried he gave her a tissue. When she really wept, he stepped outside and waited until she was ready to go on.

"It's a hard thing to find out so late you were adopted," the lawyer told Kitty.

"I think the worst of it," she said, her voice faltering, "was that I never got to thank my parents, the ones who adopted me. I would like to have thanked them for making me believe I was theirs."

The lawyer was good-natured. "You *were* theirs."

"Oh, how I loved them," Kitty said. "And I would like to have told my husband—not that it would have mattered much, but we told each other everything, you know."

Soon it was time for the lawyer to leave. "Now don't you rush, Mrs. O'Donnell, and don't give a thought to the money until you've made peace with yourself, that's just my advice. Take it or leave it."

She didn't move for a long time.

Until it was dark, and one by one, things in the kitchen began to disappear.

With the papers still spread out before her on the table, a memory came back. It was something deep and hidden, which the day's events must have dislodged.

When Kitty was nine or ten years old, she saw a woman standing at the end of her street. She had on a long coat with a belt, and her hair was pinned neatly under a hat. The street was full of children running and shouting, but the woman was looking at her. She was sure of it. Just standing there at the end of the road, staring at her. She remembered that she stopped jumping. The rope fell slack. The woman stood out against the gray, wet houses.

Kitty remembered that in the pocket of her old house-dress was a marble. She had found the marble, and wondered if it belonged to the woman, and that she had come to claim it.

Then it started to rain. But the woman in the long coat did not move. She just stood there, at the end of the road, staring as the heavy drops soaked into her clothes and the other children disappeared, one by one, into their homes.

There was family in America, the lawyer had told her, but Kitty felt it was too late, just too late for anything to be changed—except of course in her heart. That was very changed. She felt open now, to the world, to the people suffering and the places outside the village that she heard about on the news. The terrible things they went through were the things her mother must have felt too.

But as she aged, Kitty O'Donnell found herself thinking mostly about her grandfather—the man who had marched his child to the edge of the village with a gun. She thought about him a lot. She even went and found where he was buried, then lay down on the ground and put her arms around the stone where his name was written.

The Green Blanket

Mrs. Stucci had been awake since the early hours, waiting for the right moment to call her daughter. The girl was close to her father and would not take the news well.

At eight o'clock, she opened a window, and then stood with one hand on the green rotary phone, counting the hours back to the time in Los Angeles. Mrs. Stucci imagined her daughter's brown hair on the pillow. A glass of clear water on the nightstand. Her arms and legs bare under a sheet. Whether she was alone, or had a man she'd never told her mother about.

Benedetta sat up quickly when the phone rang. A dream she had been having came apart like tissue in water.

When Benedetta was in college, she'd begged to take the green rotary phone back to her sorority.

Her mother thought it was a trick. "How are we going to call you without a telephone?"

"Get a modern one, Mom, like everyone else in America."

Her father was amused. Folded his *Racing Pages* under

one arm. "She probably doesn't want us to call, did you think of that?"

Her mother couldn't believe it. "Is that true, Benedetta?"

"Of course not," she said. "I'll buy you a cordless one, then you can talk to me from any room in the house."

But Mrs. Stucci was in a bad mood because her daughter was going away again. "Your father only knows how to work the green one, Benedetta."

Mr. Stucci rubbed the bristles on his chin.

"Don't bring me into this."

The phone was on a wooden table next to a wicker chair, which was where it had always been. It was Mrs. Stucci's favorite place in the house. No one else sat there but her.

After she had spoken to her daughter for fifteen minutes, Mrs. Stucci hung up and went into the kitchen, where she took appliances and bread pans down from the cupboards.

Benedetta was coming home—not under the best circumstances—but by evening, she would be sitting on the couch helping her mother figure everything out.

Her husband, Mr. Stucci, was in the living room. He had been there all night in the same clothes since it happened. The television was on, but he was not watching it.

On the way to Los Angeles Airport, Benedetta canceled her meetings by leaving messages at offices in Century City. On the flight to JFK, she skimmed through a book on depression she had downloaded to her electronic reader.

Her father was never depressed when she was growing up. In fact he was the opposite, always seeing the bright side—even in a crisis. Perhaps all the deferred misery had built up over time and was now coming out like things stuffed into a closet for too long.

He met her mother at Catholic high school on Staten Island. They went to prom in a blue Cadillac. On the phone that morning, Benedetta learned her mother had been keeping things from her—and that for the past year, her father had been showing signs. At first he was simply reluctant to do anything outside of his routine. Mrs. Stucci thought it was fatigue—that he was finally showing his age.

Then the silences started.

Hours would go by without a word—even when Benedetta visited for Easter the year before and they made a cake. She should have noticed it then. Her once jovial father, just sitting there, staring at photographs in crumbling albums of Easters past, pointing to an image of Benedetta dressed as a rabbit, or of his wife with her hair in rollers in the back of a station wagon. That was the time they drove out to the Delaneys' in Massapequa.

Eventually her mother had to walk in and take the album away. "I need two tomatoes," she said. "Ask your daughter to go with you."

"But it's Easter, Connie, everywhere is closed."

"If a meteor were about to hit the Earth, Mr. Anthony would still be open, trust me."

Benedetta remembered it was snowing lightly. Just light

flakes falling without any sound. Her father told her to put one hand in his coat pocket like when she was a girl.

"It's good to get out of the house, Dad," she had told him.

When they got to Lorimer Meats, there was an old song playing, "Tanti Anni Fa," which her father whistled as they left the shop, each holding a tomato.

"Imagine, Benedetta—these were our hearts."

On the way home he told his daughter that if he could do life all over again, he would have gone to night school. Tried to be more than just a school bus driver.

Then he mentioned his brother Giorgio, who drowned one Sunday afternoon in the Rockaways when he was only nine. Benedetta's father was seven. He had tried to go in— but his mother grabbed both his arms.

Giorgio had almost made it. Their father got within yards before a wave tore off his glasses. Then all he could do was shout; try to dive down.

"You look at everything different when you get older," Mr. Stucci told his daughter. "So don't get old, kiddo."

There weren't many people outside. The snow had thickened and was sticking to their shoes.

As the aircraft taxied on the runway at JFK, Benedetta wondered if it could be his cholesterol medication. She would read the labels when she got there, and look things up on the Internet.

The taxi driver didn't want to go to Williamsburg,

but the airport dispatcher told him he had to if he wanted a fare.

There was so much traffic on the Cross Island Parkway, they took local streets. The overflowing trash cans, abandoned construction projects, and quick sprays of graffiti made Benedetta feel something. Made her realize how much of her life had taken place somewhere other than home.

Her mother appeared as she was paying the driver.

"He's in the living room eating Pop-Tarts."

Benedetta dragged her small suitcase up the steps.

"Have you spoken to Dr. Schillinger?"

But as they went inside, Mrs. Stucci started to cry. "I'm afraid they'll take him away."

In the sitting room, her father was exactly as her mother had described on the phone.

"Dad!" she said. But only his eyes acknowledged her.

"Oh my God! He's had a stroke. Call 911!"

But then Mr. Stucci said something.

"I haven't had a stroke." He sighed.

"Dad?"

"You live for a few years, sweetheart, and then all those memories you make as a family just wash away to nothing."

Mrs. Stucci shook her head. "He's not making any sense."

"What do you mean, Dad?"

"I just don't see the point in all of it. For all we know, we're never going to see each other again after this life, we're just gonna float around in space like dolls for all I know."

Mrs. Stucci looked at her daughter and mouthed the word "dolls" as though it were something terrifying. In the early evening she told Benedetta to go out for pasta salad.

Lorimer Meats was busy with construction workers and policemen buying packages of sausage. Then the owner appeared and asked how things were going at home.

"What do you mean?" she said.

"Well, you're here, and it's not Easter or Christmas—something must be happening."

"My father is depressed, Mr. Anthony. Nobody knows what to do with him."

Mr. Anthony asked if he had seen a doctor.

"Mom says he's seen a few. He feels that life is pointless now that he's getting older."

"Pointless?" Mr. Anthony laughed, cupping his hands. "It's all pointless. Whoever said there was a point?"

As she was leaving the shop, she heard her name being called. It was Mr. Anthony.

"I should have mentioned it to your mother before. Take your father to see Dr. Ping in Chinatown. He's an Oriental doctor."

"Ping?"

"Yeah, yeah, like Ping-Pong. Here's his card—he helped Mrs. Anthony and her last years couldn't have been brighter."

Benedetta looked at the card:

```
Dr. MO PING
EYE DOCTOR FOR HEAD CASES
"I am looking forward to you"

114 Bayard Street, 5D, New York, NY 10013
1 (212) 888-8888
52 Main Street, East Hampton, NY 11937
1 (631) 327-8888
```

When she got home, her mother studied the card while her husband was napping.

"'I am looking forward to you'?" she whispered. "What does that mean?"

"He helped Mrs. Anthony," Benedetta said.

"I don't know if your father needs an eye doctor, in Chinatown of all places, but it was thoughtful of Mr. Anthony. What did he charge you for the salad?"

Benedetta woke the next morning to the sound of her mother screaming. Mr. Stucci had gotten up in the middle of the night, gone into the attic without anyone hearing—then brought down Christmas decorations and put them all over the house.

He had even dragged in a potted tree from the porch. It stood in front of the television with lights and a fairy on top.

The most frightening part was that a Santa Claus outfit, missing for decades, had been discovered by accident and clumsily pulled on over his striped pajamas.

When Benedetta walked in, her father was sitting in his chair.

"Ho, ho, ho," he said through the ragged fibers of a fake beard.

Mrs. Stucci was crying her eyes out. "Look! Look!" she sobbed, pointing to the floor. Arranged neatly on the carpet was a small collection of Benedetta's old dolls, and a Christmas elf her father had wrapped in toilet paper.

Her mother blew her nose, then lifted her chin defiantly. "Let's try Mr. Anthony's friend, the Chinese doctor. It's time for something different."

It took a lot of convincing for Mr. Stucci to agree. He didn't even like Chinese food. In the end, Benedetta had to threaten him with taking the next flight back to Los Angeles. Within an hour, the Stucci family was in a car service halfway over the Brooklyn Bridge heading for Chinatown.

"Where's Bayard Street? the driver said indifferently. "I only know Canal Street."

"Why do you think we took a taxi?" Mrs. Stucci said indignantly. "You're supposed to know these things—it's your trade!"

Benedetta typed the address into her phone and gave the driver specific directions. They came to a stop outside a restaurant called A Palace of Lucky Dragons.

"This can't be the address," Mrs. Stucci said. "It's a place to eat." Then she looked around. "It's all restaurants here."

A Chinese man with a cane wobbled by slowly enough for Mrs. Stucci to show him the business card. The man looked at her, then raised his cane in the direction of the restaurant.

"Go through A Palace of Lucky Dragons. Office in back. Do you have appointment?"

"No, we don't," Mrs. Stucci said. "Do we need one?"

"How should I know? But Ping good; all Chinese people love Mo Ping." Then he pointed to a red Maserati parked on the street. "That's his car."

Mrs. Stucci stared at the gleaming automobile. "He must be good—you don't get something like this from being a quack."

Grabbing the tail of a golden dragon, Benedetta led her parents through the darkened restaurant. White teacups and plates were stacked up on trolleys, ready for the lunch rush.

When they reached the end of the dining room, they found a staircase. An arrow and a pair of glasses had been drawn on the wall with a black felt pen, along with the word OPEN. They followed the sign up the stairs.

The doctor's office was no bigger than their kitchen, but seating had been set up around a tattered antique barber's chair.

A pink neon sign flashed, TAKE A SEAT!

Stuck to the walls were photographs of people, post-cards, Christmas cards, and handwritten letters, which said things like:

YOU'RE THE GREATEST, DR. PING

JUST WANTED TO LET YOU KNOW HELEN
HAS RECOVERED ENOUGH TO GO
WAKEBOARDING!!!!

THANKS AGAIN FOR HELPING LITTLE JOHNNY

After ten minutes of waiting, Benedetta's father pulled his beard down and stood up.

"I want to go home," he said. "I feel worse and want to go home."

But the neon sign flashed TAKE A SEAT! TAKE A SEAT! until he sat down again.

"Just give it a few more minutes," Benedetta said.

But Mrs. Stucci was also losing steam. "We don't even know who this person is."

At that moment, a young Chinese man with a chiseled, handsome face appeared from behind a bead curtain. He was staring at the screen of a cell phone. Mrs. Stucci tapped her daughter's arm. "That must be him, Mr. Anthony's friend."

"Sorry to keep you waiting," the doctor told them, setting the phone on a shelf, "but I was on an urgent call."

"That's fine," Mrs. Stucci said. "You look very young. May I ask where you went to eye-doctor school?"

"Mom!"

Dr. Ping smiled. "You don't have to be embarrassed—I went to the International School of Insight, Beijing."

Mrs. Stucci looked at her daughter. "Sounds prestigious."

Then his phone buzzed and lit up. On the home screen was the photograph of a young, smiling blond man.

"Is that your friend?" Mrs. Stucci asked. "What nice teeth he has."

"Yes, it's my husband, Christopher."

"Congratulations," Benedetta said, before her mother had a chance to speak.

"Thanks, but let's talk about you. Mr. Anthony telephoned yesterday to say you might be coming. Usually it's best to call or text first. But rest assured, I have everything prepared for your husband."

Mr. Stucci stood up. "I don't need eyeglasses," he said. "I want to go home; it's Christmas."

Dr. Ping led him to the barber's chair.

"You're actually going home in a few minutes, Mr. Stucci, so please make yourself comfortable in the seat while we wait for the taxi."

Mr. Stucci seemed pleased.

Dr. Ping opened a wooden cabinet and carefully removed a leather case with a gold combination lock. After rolling the correct numbers, he popped the clasp and raised the lid. Inside was a vast assortment of eyeglasses, sunglasses, reading glasses, and even a few monocles.

After choosing a pair of small, red-framed children's spectacles, Dr. Ping unfolded the arms and slipped them on Mr. Stucci's head.

"How do they feel?"

Mr. Stucci was speechless.

"Dad?"

"What's happening to me? What kind of eyeglasses are these?"

"Do you want to keep them on for a moment?" Dr. Ping asked.

"Yes, I would." Then Mr. Stucci started to laugh.

A few pieces broke off the Santa Claus beard and drifted

to the floor. Mrs. Stucci stood with alarm, but Dr. Ping raised a finger to calm her.

"I can't believe it," Mr. Stucci cried. "After all these years. There's the gate and the baker coming because Uncle Pasquale ordered a cake and, my God in heaven! The ferry, and all those men in their uniforms back from the war . . . and there's my bed and Giorgio's bed, with the little hot air balloons on the blanket. I don't remember them being so small. But there's the giant Pan Am Airways poster of Hawaii, with the blue water and the girl in the coconut brassiere with flowers around her neck."

"Brassiere?" scoffed Mrs. Stucci. "Coconuts?"

"Giorgio and I used to lie on our backs imagining we was there—in Hawaii, splashing around, having the time of our lives . . . we promised to go when we were men—take our wives, drink out of shells, eat tropical clams and octopus, the real deal."

Dr. Ping gently removed the tiny spectacles from Mr. Stucci's head and put them back in the box.

"That was unbelievable!" he said. "How much are those, Doctor? Can I buy those? Can I take them home?"

"Let's try on another pair."

After taking out several candidates and inspecting them, Dr. Ping finally settled on some very old, round tortoiseshell glasses.

Mr. Stucci couldn't wait to get them on.

"Oh Jesus . . ." he said. "It's him, standing right in front of me. It's Giorgio! *Caro mio!* Giorgio!"

Mrs. Stucci grabbed her daughter's arm. "I don't like this. I'm getting chills."

"Don't worry," Dr. Ping reassured them. "This is all part of his treatment, you'll see."

"What treatment?"

"Your husband has a severe case of opticus melancholia, which if not treated can become dangerous, even fatal in some cases."

He took some ginger chews from his pocket and offered them to Mrs. Stucci and her daughter.

"The quality of a person's life in old age," Dr. Ping said, "often depends on how they see things that happened to them as children."

Mr. Stucci's cheeks were wet as Dr. Ping removed the tortoiseshell frames and gave him a tissue.

"That was a bit different, wasn't it, Mr. Stucci?"

The old man nodded. "Yes, it was, but it helped me not only remember—but feel things too. Without the feeling, memories don't mean nothing, do they, Doc?"

"Yes, I have heard that before, from other patients."

Then Mr. Stucci took off the Santa Claus beard and turned in the barber's chair to face his wife.

"Did I ever tell you that before Giorgio died, every summer, he used to sneak me into the movies? It was the only place with air-conditioning. We didn't care what the movie was. It could have been anything."

Dr. Ping cleared his throat. "Shall we continue?"

"I think he's had enough," Mrs. Stucci said.

"You couldn't possibly leave now," Dr. Ping warned them. "The treatment's only half complete."

Benedetta watched Dr. Ping search through the many pairs of glasses in his case. "How do you know which pair will fit with each patient?"

"Training."

"You seem to be very exact."

Dr. Ping smiled. "My father was the same way."

The next set was a pair of sunglasses.

"Whoa!" Mr. Stucci exclaimed. "Baby!"

Mrs. Stucci squeezed the handles of her pocketbook.

"I forgot how many guys were chasing you, Connie! And who can blame them when you put your hair up like that in a beehive?"

Mrs. Stucci blushed and touched what was left of it.

"And remember the last ferry, sweetheart? From Battery Park? The *green blanket*?"

Mrs. Stucci sat straight up in her chair. "Victor! Please!" But then the edges of her mouth curled slightly. "I thought you'd forgotten about the green blanket."

"That was the summer I taught you how to ride a scooter. We took it all the way up to the Bronx and back."

"I remember your aftershave. You got it from the drugstore in those tall bottles."

"That's right," Mr. Stucci said. "The tall ones."

"That was when you were on the school buses," Mrs. Stucci remembered, then she turned to Dr. Ping. "He was offered a promotion to management—but turned it down so he could drive Benedetta to school every morning."

· · ·

It was late afternoon when they left Chinatown. Dr. Ping said his bill would come via email. When they got home, Benedetta put all the Christmas decorations back into their boxes, while Mrs. Stucci helped her husband take off the Santa Claus outfit.

"What a day," she said. "But at least you're feeling better."

Her husband said that he was, but then an hour later they heard him moving about in the attic again.

"Oh Gawd," Mrs. Stucci said. "He probably thinks it's Thanksgiving now."

Benedetta shouted up to her father. Asked what he was doing.

"Tell your mother to pack her bags! You too!"

"Why, Dad? What's going on?"

"We're going to Hawaii."

"Who is?"

"We are!"

"When?"

"I don't know—tomorrow!"

"Dad, we can't go to Hawaii."

"But I promised my brother we'd go. It's something we have to do. I know that now."

Benedetta sighed. "Dad, I have meetings in L.A."

"Don't worry," her father called down. "Stop worrying, your mother and I have savings—we're going first-class to Honolulu in the morning! Do you think you'll want your own room at the hotel?"

"Dad, I'm thirty-seven."

Then Mrs. Stucci was standing there with her daughter, looking up through the dark opening that led to the attic.

"At least he seems more like his old self, Mom?"

"Too much like his old self!" her mother snapped; then she shouted through the square hole, "Victor, come down this instant before you get a heart attack."

"Is that you, Connie?"

"Yes, this is your wife."

"Hiya, sweetcakes."

"What are you doing up there?"

"I'm looking for something."

"Come down!"

"I'm looking for something we need to take to Hawaii."

"We're not going to Hawaii. I have to wash my hair on Thursday, and Benedetta has her job."

"What is it you're looking for, Dad?"

"A blanket," he said, "a green blanket."

Playing with Dolls

One.

They pulled into the driveway. Seeing their small home washed away some fear of what was happening. The accident was behind them now and would not come again. Chelsea was lying in the backseat of the car and everything around them was dark.

They helped their daughter through the cold air, supporting her arms in case she fell. Months ago, they had just been a small family living out their lives. Except they'd never imagined themselves like that, as if from above.

In the house, it was as though nothing had changed. The hallway looked the same. It smelled the same. The kitchen was how they remembered it. The indifference of machines maintained the illusion. But underneath, below the surface of their lives, everything had been torn out, then set back down, rootless and numb at the point of severance.

Helen used her phone to switch on the lights. She wanted it bright. Every room. Then they sat with their daughter. She had been able to undress and slip on her pajamas without help.

"You're home now," said the woman, touching the girl's hair, pushing it back with her hand. Encircling them were

Chelsea's things. A plastic cup of crayons, pretend jewelry, ticket stubs, a program from theater camp, and drawings.

A test would be if Chelsea remembered which doll was her favorite, and which had not been touched for a long time. She had always played with dolls. They sat primly in a row, as if on display in a museum of childhood.

When she was in bed, the new Chelsea finally spoke, her first full sentence. "I was in the hospital two days. Why are you making such a big deal?"

Her parents looked at one another because it was *exactly* how Chelsea spoke. Maybe this was going to work after all, they thought.

But it was just the beginning.

"Don't you feel tired from the medicine, Chelsea?" the woman asked.

She shook her head.

"Hungry then?"

Chelsea looked around at her possessions. "Just confused."

Her father was sitting at the bottom of the girl's bed, his fingers spread on the covers. "Can you tell us what you're confused about?"

She didn't know, just that everything seemed different in a way she couldn't understand.

"Well, it *is* late," said the woman sensibly. When no one responded, she looked out toward the garden, but was unable to see beyond a perfect square of night. She imagined where the plants and the trees were supposed to be—how darkness was simply the absence of something else; an emptiness to be filled with fear.

"Are you sure you're not thirsty?" said the mother, turning to her husband. "What did the doctor say she can drink?"

"Mom," Chelsea pleaded, "stop."

There was nothing else to do now but let her sleep.

Tomorrow would be a different country. They would have to stay together, to find their way.

The girl's father tapped the covers out of habit, only realizing after what a risk he had taken. It was a gesture only Chelsea could have known. But slowly a foot appeared from under the comforter.

"Thanks, Dad," the girl said, as her father began to massage, mechanically at first, as though he were afraid. He couldn't believe the foot was warm as though full of *her* blood.

"Not *too* hard," said the girl's mother.

They had made it home and their new lives had begun.

Two.

The official adjustment period was three months. On the morning of the first day home, the girl woke and found that John and Helen had cooked *her* favorite things. There were waffles, everything bagels, turkey bacon, and French toast. Even flowers in a vase of cold, still water. The woman must have gone out early.

Her parents stopped talking when they saw her. They wanted to know if she had slept well.

"Fine," she said, but not coming any closer to them.

"That's good," said her mother. "Your own bed, after all."

"That's *very* good," the father agreed. "We slept too."

"You're home now," said her mother, blinking her eyes. "Oh, I feel so blessed."

The girl just looked at them. "Why are you both here?"

John and Helen had not anticipated direct questions. But it was just like Chelsea. Just like her. And that reassured them in a way her physical presence had failed to.

In the end it was the mother that answered.

"Your father and I have taken three months each off work."

Chelsea was barefoot and stepped over cool tiles to the refrigerator. "When do I go back to school?"

"The doctor suggested it," said her father. "So we could be together after what happened."

Chelsea fumbled with a large carton of juice. John and

Helen resisted the urge to intervene as orange liquid plopped into a tall glass.

"But I'm fine."

"Don't you feel exhausted?" asked her mother. "I would."

"No," Chelsea said, "I feel normal."

The woman studied the long, burned strips of turkey bacon on the plate before her.

Chelsea frowned. "You seem disappointed, Mom. Do you want me to feel bad or something?"

Her father had been studying her this whole time. "Don't be silly. Last night you said you were confused."

"I'm fine now."

"You've been in the hospital," said her mother. "There were machines and tubes coming out of you."

"I am fine now."

"That's for the doctors to decide," her father said with forced calmness, "and they said three months."

The girl sat down with the man and woman at the table. They watched her eyes move across the landscape of things to eat.

"When do I get friends?" the girl said, then corrected herself without hesitation. "When do I get to see my friends?"

"Three months," said her mother, looking now at the waffles. It was a lie, and her husband knew it was a lie. But there had been no time to discuss the future before she was ready to bring home.

Chelsea slammed down her glass. "What?"

Her mother reached out, but the girl pulled her hand back. "When can I have my phone and VR glasses?"

The girl's parents knew for sure now she didn't remember the accident. They were hoping she would. It would help her understand why they were being so careful.

"I'm sorry," said her father, "but texting, video chat, and virtual reality are just not allowed."

"Even *Movie-Me* streaming?" said the girl, who had spent hours with her friends watching popular films with their own faces and bodies digitally traced over the faces and bodies of the original actors.

"Even *Movie-Me*," said her mother, "but you can stream as many regular films as you like, because for the next three months, you've got no homework or chores."

"You're kidding?"

"Isn't that great?"

"Why would I want to watch a film if I can't put me or my friends in it? That's the whole point."

"Sorry," said her father, "but we're serious—no contact with anyone but us for three months."

Another lie, but at least they'd have time to sort something out. The doctor had said there would be many things to organize and come to terms with.

"But you can binge watch *anything*," her mother said. "We can do it together."

The father picked up a piece of cut fruit. Examined it in his hands. "I can't wait. It will be like old times."

But Chelsea's mood was sour. "What old times?"

"When you were young," her father said brightly.

Chelsea carefully picked on a waffle. "I hated being young."

Her mother stood quickly from the breakfast table; her bottom lip was shaking. "Do you even remember that? Do you?" The woman's face wrinkled, as though collapsing. She reached very slowly for Chelsea's hair. But the child rose too, ignoring the hand, choosing instead to meet the woman's anger. "When can I have my phone!"

Then they heard the man's voice. "Everything will be fine once we get used to this."

Chelsea sighed through her smart braces, as they changed color from silver to neon blue. "Why are you both being so weird?"

"Try and remember one movie," her father said, "your favorite movie, Chelsea."

But the girl was defiant, which in its own way placated their fears.

"I don't have a favorite because I never got to choose."

"That's not true," said her mother, still standing over the girl.

"Yes, it is; anything I love, you hate."

"She's right, Helen," the man said with a pleased look. "She's got a point there—we never let her watch anything scary."

The woman nodded without speaking. For her there was nothing scarier than what was happening to them now.

Then the father said, "Maybe she can pick out a horror film she's always wanted to see? Something that'll really frighten us."

"Seriously, Dad?"

"You're home now," said her mother, "this is where you belong, and where we all have to recover from what's happened."

The second night in her bed, the girl started screaming. Her father was first in the room. "Chelsea," he said, touching her arm, ". . . it's just a bad dream, Chelsea, wake up."

They knew she was out of it when terror bunched into heavy, gasping sobs, as though each wave of emotion were being pulled, with great force, from somewhere, far away.

Her mother stroked the girl's forehead, feeling that inside every child is someone very small and without language; a stowaway from long ago.

The woman could see this little girl now. Could feel her presence with them, in the room. A measure of what was lost.

Three.

In the morning her father filled the sink with hot water. He dipped a cloth and spread the steaming towel on his face. He rinsed the shaving brush and made lather in a bowl. Then he began scraping at the small hairs. After, he pulled up handfuls of cold water onto his cheeks. Combed his hair. Splashed aftershave from a blue bottle.

Chelsea's mother wanted to clean. It was the morning of the third day. She started with the windows. But there were fingerprints and breath marks from before the accident. And while sweeping she found hairs, skin flakes, a smile of toenail—but the woman kept moving, kept turning her hands in circles, trying to rub away the tiny parts of their old selves.

Chelsea was silent. In her room wearing headphones, listening to music on an ancient MP3 player. In the afternoon, they ate pizza and watched a horror film about a child who lived in the walls of an old house and couldn't love anyone without eventually killing them.

The next day, the girl stayed in her room. At lunchtime her parents knocked and entered with a plate of cookies and something to drink. On the floor were their daughter's favorite books and a drawing pad. A few colored markers had rolled to the edges of where she was sitting, cross-legged, staring at photographs of summer camp. Chelsea had been drawing from the pictures. She had made girls from black

47

lines, then filled their bodies with colored ink. Each girl had a cell phone, and there were bubbles filled with writing.

Her father was the first to notice her dolls were missing from their usual place on the shelf. In a corner of the room was a pile of shoes and dresses, which the girl had covered up with pieces of paper ripped from her pad. For a year, the dolls had not been taken down. Their daughter had been opening herself to the world, and no longer needed her imagination to make things come alive. When they didn't leave, the girl went back to coloring. Her parents looked around for the dolls, but couldn't see where they were.

After a whole week of meals on trays and single-syllable answers—the woman said it felt as if they were living out the same day over and over again. When they heard Chelsea's music through the door, they knew it was safe to talk.

"She's not comfortable with us, John, and that's why she's barricaded herself in there."

"She just wants to be in her room—like any thirteen-year-old."

"Something is very wrong with that child."

"Of course it's wrong," said the woman, "that's why we're here."

Helen looked at her hands. The skin on them was dried out from cleaning.

Her husband touched them. "I think we might be scaring her, Helen, I think that might be it."

"I feel she's indifferent to us."

"Well we're her parents, and it's only the trial period."

Helen clenched her teeth. Made an effort to swallow the

feeling that was clawing its way to her mouth. After some moments, she managed to release the words calmly, though it shocked her to hear them out loud.

"I feel like I'm betraying our *real* daughter," she said, remembering hair and nails in the dustpan, "that she's lost and we're not looking for her."

This comment seemed to surprise the father, as though it were *his* faith he'd imagined breaking first. After all, he had witnessed more than his wife. Even now, when his eyes were closed, he could still see the pieces of their child under plastic sheets. But since coming home, he had been learning to impersonate the man he remembered before the accident. Helen had stayed upstairs in the hospital ward, where Chelsea's torso and head were tangled in tubes and wires, suspending her between this world and others, in a place they couldn't get to.

Her brain was active, the doctors knew that for certain. But Chelsea couldn't breathe without a machine pushing air into her lungs, then pulling it out. And she would never wake up. There was no chance of that.

At night, with the ward in darkness, when they were alone, John listened. Got close with his head down. Pretended Chelsea was asleep and just listened.

They could still hear Chelsea's music through the door of her bedroom. John made something hot to drink and they sat down.

"Maybe if we hadn't been told," he said, "it might be working."

"But we were told, John."

They looked at Chelsea's bedroom door, to make sure it was still closed.

"But if no one had been told," her husband said again, "then it really could be like it was before."

His wife's face hardened. "It will never be like before, and neither will we."

"It could be if you let it."

"I can't, John, that's the point."

Her husband felt something fiery rise into his mouth.

"Listen to me," he said with more gentleness than he had intended, "what else can we do? This was the only option, you know that."

Outside a motorcycle went past, shifting clumsily through the gears. Then suddenly, Chelsea was standing there, in her bedroom doorway. Her mother jumped up.

"What's happening?" she said. "Why is Mom crying?"

"Mom is just upset about what happened."

Chelsea had on denim overalls and was barefoot. John could see that she had painted her toenails with colored markers. Some of the ink had gotten on her skin. It was a normal thing, except now it felt garish.

The doctor said they would know after three months if it were possible to go on.

They ate leftover pizza for dinner and watched another film. This one was about a fox trying to feed his family with stolen chickens.

When John put Chelsea to bed, she asked if Mom was really okay.

"She will be," her father said, not really believing it.

"But why is this all such a big deal? I'm totally fine."

The doctor, a woman called Irene, had warned them the girl would remember only being in the hospital for a day or two. John looked deep into the eyes of the child, trying to find a tunnel that would lead him somewhere familiar. He *knew* a part of him could believe it, could *really* do it with enough practice. What was truth anyway—but an excuse for violence?

He touched the girl's forehead. "Just don't worry, Chelsea. We're going to do our best."

"Why can't I go back to school? I want my life back, Dad."

"This is your life now. In this house with us, your mom and dad."

"But what's wrong with me? Am I dying or something?" Her eyes moved from side to side.

John laughed to break his expression of shock. "We're all going to die, someday."

"Then why is Mom being weird?"

"She's overwhelmed. We almost lost you."

"Well, you're acting like I died or something."

John took a deep breath.

"Do you remember dying?"

"Just the bus stop," the girl said, her cheeks turning red. She seemed about to cry. John wondered if he should call his wife in. This was so much like their daughter. "I was wearing my virtual reality glasses," she confessed, leaning forward, putting both arms around her father. "I know you told me I couldn't because it's dangerous, and I'm sorry, I'm *so* sorry, Daddy."

She lay back down and looked into her father's face. "That's why you won't let me have them, isn't it? Because I disobeyed you and Mom by wearing my virtual reality glasses?"

"Don't worry about that now, Chelsea, it's too late—just try and tell me what you remember after the bus stop."

John braced for the answer, watching the girl search her memories and pull words together.

"Just waking up in the hospital with you and Mom staring at me."

"Then you're lucky," he said, trying to keep his breathing steady. "We're all lucky actually."

"Am I different since the accident, Dad?"

"It doesn't matter," John told her. "We're going to love you no matter what."

Four.

The next day, John found his wife in the hallway still wearing her nightgown. She was looking at photographs they had put in frames, moving slowly across the wall of faces, each one now anchored to a different moment of grief.

"If you're trying to find imperfections, you won't," John said gently.

It was early. Chelsea was still sleeping.

"You sound like them."

"Whatever they did worked."

"Well, it's not working for me."

Her honesty made him angry. But he held his temper to prevent her courage from turning to recklessness. "I meant physically, Helen."

He looked past his wife's head at a picture of Chelsea on the beach as a toddler. She had on a white cotton hat with ruffles. Her arms and legs were like pink sausages under the shade of a beach umbrella. She was bending to look at something outside the frame. She was young then and couldn't speak. The emotion and curiosity was in her face, yet to be culled by language. John laid both hands on his wife's shoulders.

"Can't we just try, Helen?"

She pulled away bitterly. "I am trying! Isn't that obvious?"

"But she's exactly the same, she—"

"Not to me, John—I'm her mother, remember?"

"Well, you're not really acting like it."

Helen turned. Her face looked cold and haggard.

"Because it feels like a betrayal."

"You have to make yourself believe it, Helen—that's how it works. Come on . . . give yourself permission to be happy again. There's no other way."

Her face dropped the way it had at the hospital, into a shapeless agony. It reminded John of the giant theatrical mask on the entrance gates to their daughter's summer theater camp.

"I don't think I can go on."

"You have to, Helen, or this family will break apart."

"Because of me?"

"Because of your unwillingness to love."

"But that's the point—I feel the exact opposite. Like loving is the worst thing I could do."

"But why?"

"Because it would mean the love before meant nothing."

But love is love, he wanted to say.

They steered their eyes back to the pictures that now seemed to mock them.

"I don't know what's worse," she said, "grief or guilt."

"She can never find out—you have to promise me that."

"That's the worst part," said his wife. "Think how she'd suffer if she knew, John."

"But that's good! Doctor Irene said *that* was part of the plan—for us to worry about her suffering means we love her."

Helen nodded, but after a moment said, "I think we need to leave this house."

"The doctor recommended three months."

"I know, but staying inside like this is not helping."

"Where will we go?"

"It doesn't matter—but we need to do something, as a family."

"Okay," John said, "that I can understand."

He made some coffee and called Chelsea from her room. Talked about where they would go.

"What are we running away from now?" she said.

"It's something we need to do," Helen told her.

"I'll check the charge on the car tonight," John added, "and fill the microfridge with infused water."

"How come I can go out, but not go back to school? My friends will think I'm dead! When can I go back to school? Tell me!"

The voice was familiar, but her insistence felt sinister, beyond what was normal. Helen stood quickly, spilling her coffee. "You aren't going back to school, for God's sake! How many times do we have to tell you that? Christ!"

The skin tightened on the girl's face. The mother and father waited but she did not speak. There was no sound. Only her eyes were moving.

John spoke then, afraid of what might be going on inside their daughter.

"Please go into your room, Chelsea. Mom and I will figure this out."

Helen watched her go, then turned to her husband. "Our *real* daughter would never, ever, *ever* behave like that."

John sat very still as the words cut through him. "Maybe that's because her *real* mother would never have spoken to her like that."

"Jesus Christ," she said. "You're a bastard, John, a real bastard."

He got up then and went out of the room. She could hear his feet on the stairs. Then a door closing. She was alone with the stained tablecloth and her ragged breathing. She sat like that for a long time, feeling as though all she had to do was pull out the tangle of her insides and discard them.

But over dinner the mood was different. Helen complimented Chelsea on her manners, and on a drawing she had made. It showed a girl standing on a cliff edge looking out to sea.

John kissed his wife on the head when he rose to collect dishes. She touched his hand.

For one meal, it seemed as though they might be able to go on.

Over dessert, Helen asked where they were going.

"The sea," John said.

"You loved the beach," said her mother.

"In the summer," Chelsea said, "not now."

John tried to keep the good mood going. "It's nice all year-round, just different."

"How come I can go to the beach but not to school?"

"It's just a day," Helen said, her voice hoarse from crying. "We can always stay in the car if it's too much."

"It's settled," John said. "Tomorrow, we're going for a family day at the seaside."

That night, Helen and John had sex for the first time since their daughter's accident. It was quick and hard, as though they were trying to break through the rubble of emotions that had accumulated between them. After, they held hands and imagined the sea. How the endless water would make them feel.

Five.

Some time ago, about a month after the accident, John and Helen drove from their home to a part of the hospital where the incubation labs were housed. At first they wanted to touch it—touch her. But it wasn't *her* yet. The body looked exactly the same. Every scar, every freckle—even tiny craters on her knees from where she had fallen off her tricycle. The technician told them the body was woven from a fabric that was grown. The blood had some elements of real blood to prevent hemophilia. The company kept an Italian artist on staff, to check the skin pigmentation and other things only an artist might see. John remembered him from the e-brochure. The artist had long hair and wore a scarf.

They would be one of the first families to try the new technology, which was why it had been offered at no cost. The company was financed in part by the drone industry, and staffed by medical engineers and marketing gurus. The chief physician, Dr. Irene Weber, had promised that, despite the graphic nature of the accident, the company had paid for a media blackout, so that Chelsea would not accidentally stumble upon anything, if she found a way to go online.

The immediate goal was for her to *really* feel and *really* live.

"What if she finds out," Helen asked, "or realizes she's not growing up, what then?"

"Call me Irene," said the doctor. "To be honest, Helen, we don't know. She might not notice she's not aging if she feels okay."

"Well then, it's lucky we live on a desert island, where she'll have no other children to compare herself to." They should have known then it wasn't going to work.

The doctor nodded. "I understand your fears, but remember that while she'll look the same, she's capable of learning."

"How so?" John asked.

"Everything has been copied exactly; that means all neuronal activity recorded, simulated, and—most important—*sequenced* to establish a precedent for any future stimuli."

They didn't speak on the way home. Over the freeway, drones were still whizzing about, guided by their onboard GPS and local sonar. New laws had promised no-fly zones over areas of population movement, but nothing was being enforced. Anyone shooting them out of the sky was quickly sentenced.

The collision had occurred between 8:02 and 8:03 in the morning. A delivery quad-copter collided with the top of a Dutch elm tree and veered up into the sky, where it clipped the blade of a yellow filter drone as it sucked in the morning's excess pollen. Both machines immediately stopped functioning and began falling to earth. Six seconds later, the delivery quad-copter hit the top of a bus and shattered, while the filter drone—about the size of a small car—smashed into the sidewalk, where one of its blades broke off and shredded a thirteen-year-old girl wearing headphones and a virtual reality mask. Then the drone pollen sac burst, and everything was covered with yellow dust.

The girl knew she had been hit by something when her head hit the sidewalk. Her last thought was the kind of panic all children feel when they know they're in trouble.

Six.

The weather cooperated.

After breakfast, they filled a cotton bag with fruit, chocolate, and towels. John put on shorts and suede loafers.

They took the main road, then turned off for the beach.

It was a mild day, and there weren't many people. Just a few pensioners sitting in their cars. The lifeguard drones were up on their platforms, ever alert to the sights and sounds of human distress.

Helen and Chelsea took off their shoes.

"Can I do a cartwheel, Mom?"

Her mother smiled for the first time since the girl had come home. "Have fun," she told her, "that's why we're here."

"Can I run too?"

"Anything you want," said her mother. John and Helen linked arms and watched the girl get farther and farther away. The sand was soft under their feet and waves were folding gently in the distance.

"Are you sure it's a good idea? Letting her do that?" John said, but when he turned, he saw his wife's cheeks were glistening.

"It doesn't matter anymore, John."

"Why is that?"

"Because she's not our daughter."

He felt too afraid to argue, and instead tried to draw attention to what was happening around them. "I think a day out like this will make us all feel better."

But Helen was determined and said everything she felt. After listening, the man's legs began shaking. He went down on the sand, trying to breathe normally, but never taking his eyes off the child. The woman stood over him.

"How long could we have kept it going, John?"

He didn't answer. He couldn't. The way he was sitting made him look like a small boy, when all the decisions of his life were made by others.

"And how would we explain to her why she's not getting any older? Why she isn't menstruating? Real people grow up, John, they change. This isn't real, it's fantasy; it's trying to love a photograph that doesn't realize it's a photograph."

"But she believes it, Helen; she *feels* alive."

His wife got down next to her husband, put an arm around his shoulders. "That's why I called the doctor yesterday."

"Yesterday?"

"When you were up in our room."

"What for?"

"I think you know what for," she said, stroking his hand. He was no longer looking at the distant figure of their child, but at the white triangle of a sail. A boat at sea in the afternoon.

"When?"

"Today."

"You don't want a bit longer?"

"I can't, John. It's an agony beyond what I thought I could handle."

"Are you sure this is what you want?"

Helen turned her entire body toward her husband, then cried the way she had cried when the police came to their door that first morning.

As though sensing her distress, the girl, far away now, stopped doing cartwheels and looked at them from across the galaxy of tiny grains.

"Helen," John said looking up, "she's watching us, Helen."

His wife took her arm back and waved.

"You're amazing!" she shouted. "So amazing!"

The girl must have heard because she attempted a cartwheel from a standing position but fell down on the sand.

"I'm sorry, John. I can't hide my grief anymore."

"She wouldn't have expected you to."

"Who?"

"Chelsea," he said. "I mean, if she were watching us now, her spirit, she might be happy we had found some comfort."

"That's exactly the problem," Helen confessed, "there's no comfort for me, there's nothing, less than nothing. How do I mourn for someone I'm not allowed to admit has gone?"

"I get it," John told her, "but she wouldn't have been mad at us for trying."

"No," Helen said. "She would have understood everything we're going through. She was great like that."

After a few long seconds, John forced the words out.

"I think I'm ready."

"Are you sure? Because it's something we have to do

together. We have twenty-four hours from the time I called Irene yesterday to stop the experiment."

He helped his wife up and they walked toward the water. They went quickly without speaking.

There were rocks near the water's edge, like molars from the mouth of an old god. Chelsea had rolled up her pants and was standing in a rock pool.

"The water is so warm!" she said. "Come on, Dad—you're in shorts, join me."

"Wow, it *is* warm," he said, stepping in.

Helen was wearing pants but went in anyway. Chelsea was delighted and clapped her hands. Her parents did not look at the water—at life momentarily stranded—but at the girl before them, who was startled by the sudden intensity of their gaze.

"Why are you guys looking at me like that?"

"We just love you, is all," Helen said, keeping hold of John's hand.

"You're being weird again," Chelsea told them. Then something shot across the pool, just below the surface of the water. "There it is! That's the fish I was trying to show you!"

"Come and sit with us on the sand," said the girl's mother.

"Are you crazy? I have to see where the fish went—and the sand is all wet."

"Come and sit on a rock then," said the girl's father. "Look—there's a smooth one."

"But I'm trying to find this fish . . ."

"He'll always be there," her mother said, "waiting for

you in his little house. We want to talk to you about going back to school tomorrow, and getting your phone back. We think you're ready, but need to talk about it."

Chelsea, smiling now, stepped out of the rock pool. John had taken off his jacket and made a cushion for her.

"There's something we need to tell you," he said.

Chelsea shuffled uncomfortably between them. "Is it about the accident?"

"No," said her mother, "forget about that."

"Am I going to die or something?" Chelsea said, still out of breath from seeing a fish and the excitement that life might go back to normal.

"You're not going to die," her father said, surprised at how calm he felt now the moment was upon them; how easily it was to lie, even though, until that moment, everything they had ever done, had ever thought, had ever seen, was a deception of sorts.

"We just want to remind you of something," said her mother.

Chelsea rolled her eyes. "That you love me, I know."

"Just go along with it, please," her father said, "because we're your parents and it would make us happy."

"Go along with what?"

"I want to say a prayer."

"Why, Mom? What for? You don't believe in God."

"Well, we don't know what's out there, Chelsea. For all I know, there might be spirits watching us this very minute."

John took the hand of his daughter that was closest to him. Helen took the other. In their minds were many thoughts, feelings, and pictures—but like all memories, too fleeting and esoteric to be captured and shared.

They rubbed the child's hands the way they had been shown on the dummy. They rubbed and they stroked the child's hands together, with a pressure and motion that would verify them as authorized users and commence shutdown.

Chelsea closed her eyes. "That feels good," she said, "whatever you're doing."

"Can you hear the sea, Chelsea?"

"You mean the waves? They're making me tired."

"I think it's time we all had a nap," said her mother. John nodded because he was unable to speak then.

"What about the fish, Mom?"

"He'll find his way home when the tide comes in," said her mother, "that's what always happens."

They stayed until the tide splashed over their shoes.

The adventure of the last few weeks had come to an end. Now it was a matter of learning to live with love that kept blowing back into their faces, like an unbearable heat.

John carried the girl's body across the sand. He wondered if people would think she had drowned in the sea. But there was only one person in the parking lot when they got there, and she thought the child was sleeping.

They laid her down in the backseat of the car, using towels to make sure she wouldn't roll on the floor when they started driving. Her eyes were closed and her mouth hung open.

John wanted to go in the backseat and hold her on the

journey back. But Helen's hands were shaking so she couldn't drive. In their heads lingered the sound of her final words. Not the meaning of the words, but the sound of them, the music that gives language meaning.

When John started the engine, Helen reached over and turned it off. "I don't trust them," she said, "not to wake her up again."

"Why would they?"

"To find out where they went wrong."

"She'd ask for us. She'd think she was Chelsea."

"That's exactly what I mean."

So they waited for the last person to leave the parking lot. Then they filled the car with driftwood and set it alight.

When the fire really took, the whole vehicle was engulfed. They had to stand back as flames rolled, crackling through the backseat.

When they were sure, Chelsea's mother and father turned away from the blaze and started the long walk home. Their clothes were full of burning. The air felt hollow without the flames crackling before them.

"I can't go through this again," John said. "I can't ever go through this again."

"You won't," Helen told him. "It's over now."

But a year later Helen was pregnant, and their lives began where all the old ones had come to an end.

The Pigeon

A rthur left school when he was sixteen to focus on fighting. He told his mother he had one chance to live his dream, to do something spectacular. She stitched his shorts when they ripped, and in golden thread embroidered his nickname, *The Pigeon*.

He would soon be facing his toughest opponent, and as his hands were wrapped and taped each morning, Arthur thought of all the people he hated. The man who'd hit his mother in the supermarket, their old landlord, and three boys Arthur had met years before—though one was already dead, his body discovered by workers in a Newark rail yard.

When a famous cut man called Lenny DeJesus told Arthur that all the shadowboxing, jump rope, pad work, situps, sparring, and fancy footwork meant nothing if he didn't eat right, Arthur went to the library with his mother.

Side by side they turned each page. Plates of glistening meat and fish. Perfect meals that could never be eaten. Arthur learned how to make soup from bones. The right time to sprinkle herbs from France that came in a little bag and looked like drugs.

His mother had false teeth, so Arthur discovered a way to soften meat by soaking it overnight in sauce before cooking it.

"If the fighting doesn't work out, you could always be a chef," she said, watching her son sprinkle capers into a bubbling sauce.

Arthur gave her a look.

"I mean when you retire from boxing."

"As world champion."

His mother nodded. "You're already world champion to me."

Arthur sighed, but the words found their place very deep inside, where they would stay for a long time.

Most evenings, he watched old fights and training videos posted online. Some were in other languages, and some showed lives of despair. He explained to his mother that featherweights had hand speed and agility, while the heavyweights were prizefighters that drew the big crowds.

Mike Tyson was Arthur's favorite because of what he said about "bad intentions." Any boxer without them had no chance in the ring. Arthur could feel his—a persistent viciousness just below the surface of his life, like his heart was a cage of dogs with their mouths snapping. When he told his mother about these feelings, she cried and said if he ever went to jail she would die of heartbreak. But he wanted her to understand it was part of who he was.

As a boy, Arthur had struggled to keep his weight down. He walked to school even though it took longer. He didn't like the bus. Once, a girl knocked his glasses off.

His best friend was a pigeon. Arthur kept Sam in a coop he'd made from chicken wire and an orange crate.

When Arthur was twelve, three boys broke into the yard looking for things to steal. One of the boys held Arthur, while another took Sam and wrung his neck. On the ground his body looked like a gray rag. Arthur missed school the next day and buried Sam in Central Park near the pond where there were ducks. That evening he walked around the neighborhood with a knife in his pocket.

A week before Arthur's big fight—a championship bout that would be live on Spanish-language television—he was training fiercely and trying to make weight. One night, after eight rounds of sparring, Arthur left the gym later than usual—too tired even to stuff his sweaty gloves with newspaper or rinse his mouthpiece. Outside it was all buses and gypsy cabs. A few people walked in heavy coats. He imagined getting right into bed, but knew he had to eat again, because Wednesday was roadwork.

He mostly ran in Central Park, timed laps around the pond. And there were always girls out after school—and serious runners he could use to test himself. Sometimes he went straight down Fifth Avenue past the synagogue, and the museums, and the doorman buildings where he wanted his mother to live when he was world champion.

As Arthur skipped down the subway steps, hoping to

hear a train grinding in, a tall figure came quickly toward him with something held up.

"C'mon," the man said, twisting a knife in the air. "You know what this is."

Arthur dropped his gym bag and took two steps back. His pulse quickened, and blood drained from his hands the way it always did before a fight. Then he heard his own voice: a hard monologue urging him to get inside—past the reach of the knife—with some quick combination that was on target. Knockout punches don't come from power, but from turning the head so the neck whips. Arthur rolled his fingers into tight fists. But then something unexpected happened. Arthur noticed the thief was wearing the exact same hooded sweatshirt that he had on under his puffy coat. They had been heaped in a cardboard bin at Kingdom of Sports on Black Friday; Arthur had grabbed one just in time.

An express train rattled through the station and in the friction of steel, Arthur heard his mother's cries when she told him she would die of heartbreak.

He reached into his pants and pulled out his wallet. It was brown leather. A gift from last Christmas. He knew it was something fancy when he saw the Macy's bag under the tree with his name on the tag. He tossed it on the ground.

As the robber bent down, Arthur saw they were about the same age, but the thief was taller, with a long face and dull, unblinking eyes. He put Arthur's wallet in the front pocket of his hoodie and backed away with the knife held up.

When the thief was almost out of sight, Arthur shouted,

"Hey, stop!" The man turned uneasily. "If you're going to be out robbing people tonight—you're gonna need a coat." Without thinking, Arthur rolled out of his black jacket and threw it down.

The thief's voice seemed too deep for his body. "You tryin' to trick me or somethin', man?"

"Take the coat," Arthur said. "Pick it up."

The man came back and scooped the jacket off the ground in one motion, then began shuffling toward an exit on the south side.

When the thief was almost at the steps, Arthur shouted something else. "You eaten tonight?" The footsteps stopped.

"No," came a faint reply.

Arthur picked up his gym bag and moved confidently toward where the thief was waiting. "Well, c'mon then," he said, passing him for the stairs. When he reached the top step, the thief began to follow, then caught up as Arthur crossed the street and neared the heavy doors of an all-night diner.

The two men entered and slid into a booth. A woman at a nearby table was putting on lipstick using the camera on her phone as a mirror. Her hair looked wet, but it was just the way she had styled it.

The thief sat across from Arthur. The coat was too small and made him look like a boy who was growing too fast. Arthur watched him take it off. Then a waiter came with two menus.

"Hey, champ!" he said. "We got your egg whites already whisk', and the milk is fresh from the cow."

Arthur pointed at the thief. "This is my friend, Marcus."

The waiter stuck the pen behind his ear. "I can tell," he said, looking at their matching sweatshirts. "Twins, right?"

Arthur laughed, but the thief just sat there, as if waiting for something to happen.

"I'll take an egg white omelet, with mushrooms and peppers," Arthur said.

"Home fries?"

Arthur shook his head. "Trying to make weight for the big fight."

The waiter turned to the thief. "How about you, boss?"

"Uh, I'll have the same thing."

"You want home fries?"

"He's hungry," Arthur said. "Give him double."

"You wan' a Coke to drink or something?"

"Yeah, a Coke," said the thief.

"Ice and *limón*?"

"Okay."

The waiter wrote it down on his pad and went away.

"Marcus?" the thief said to Arthur. "My name ain't Marcus."

Arthur could smell food cooking and it made him feel good.

"What was I gonna say? Robber? Gangster? Hustler? Pimp daddy?"

The thief smiled. "Why you being so nice to me, man? You from a church or something?"

Arthur looked down at his hands. His knuckles were thick and ached with chronic bruising.

"No, I'm a fighter. Twelve–oh, with ten knockouts in the first round. Got my thirteenth coming up. Title fight."

The thief stirred in his seat. "For a second I thought you was gonna fight me."

"Yeah," Arthur said, "me too, but now we're just two guys sitting down to a meal."

It surprised him how much he sounded like his mother.

When the food was brought over, they ate quickly without speaking. The thief opened his omelet and removed the peppers one by one. Arthur watched him pile them on the toast plate, beside foil squares of butter that shimmered.

Then one of the dishwashers came out. He was sixteen, but had crossed the border from Mexico when he was thirteen. The dishwasher's overalls were wet from pulling racks out of the machine. Arthur told him to slide into the booth. Then the waiter came over with black coffee and more Coke for the thief.

"When you're not working," Arthur said to the dishwasher, "come by the gym and I'll train you a little. Cleaning pots gives you strong shoulders."

The boy smiled and drank his coffee.

Then the thief leaned forward. "*Dia libre*," he told the dishwasher, "*vete al gimnasio*. You understand?"

When they had finished their coffee and the boy was back in the kitchen, Arthur asked the thief why he was robbing people if he could speak another language.

"There's a word for that," Arthur said. "It's bilingual. And if you know two languages, why not five? Why not twenty?"

The thief laughed.

"I ain't kidding. What's your real name?"

The thief went to speak, and Arthur realized he had a stutter.

"William."

"Billy?"

"Yeah."

"Like Billy Graham—New York fighter from back in the day—defeated Sugar Ray when they were our age. He had 102 wins in his career."

"How many you got?"

"Twelve, but like I told you, I got a big one coming up—you wanna come watch? I can get you ringside."

The thief shuffled in his seat. "I was trying to rob you, man—"

Arthur felt confidence surge through him. "Well, you ain't dead, you ain't in jail, maybe it's time for a second chance?"

"I don't deserve no second chance," he scoffed.

Arthur hesitated, wondering if he'd killed anyone during a robbery, or if he was in a gang. But the words came out anyway.

"It's never too late, William. Where you live at?"

"With my uncle, but he wants me out."

"Why?"

"'Cause his girl told him she didn't want no kids."

"How old are you?"

"Fifteen."

"Your folks still around?"

"My mother, she in Virginia with her third husband and his kids, and I don't know my father."

"Me neither," Arthur said, "poor guy."

"How you figure that?"

"On account of how sorry he'll be when I'm world champ, and got the Lambo, fly crib on Fifth Ave., fur coats, artworks and shit . . ."

William smiled. "You got big dreams, man, respect."

"What about your dreams?"

"I'm just trying to keep goin'."

"I could teach you how to fight. You got reach; that's a big plus. Maybe I could get you a few bucks sweeping up the locker room."

"I don't like fightin'."

"Serious?"

They were both laughing now.

"Then why you doin' what you do?"

"To eat, man—my uncle don't give me shit, and I gotta save up for when he kick me out."

Arthur looked at their clean plates. At the pile of peppers on a side dish made by the thief.

"Go back to school then."

"I can't—you know how it is."

"Yeah," Arthur said, remembering the boys who had killed his pigeon. He wondered if William had a heart of snarling dogs. But then felt he didn't. That it was most likely an empty place, never really lived in.

When the waiter came with the check in a plastic tray, William didn't realize and just sat there.

Eventually, Arthur had to say something. He thought the thief would laugh again, but instead he blushed, then reached inside his hoodie and put the brown billfold on the table. Arthur took it and laid some bills in the tray. There were also mints. Christmas candies. Hard white circles with green stripes. Arthur wondered where the uncle's home was—if William had a room and if his bed was made up, or if the blankets were rough and unwashed. If he had posters on the walls of people cut out from magazines—or if the paint was peeling and there were damp circles where the plaster had swollen with mold. Arthur took the emergency twenty-dollar bill hidden between his bus pass and tattered photographs of his mother, Sam the pigeon, and Mike Tyson.

"Whatcha doin'?" the thief said, looking around. "Why you giving me money?"

"I'm not giving it to you—I want to buy your knife."

When Arthur got home that night his mother was falling asleep in front of the television. She had on a bathrobe and looked worn out.

"I was worried about you," she said. "What time is it?"

"You don't have to worry about me," Arthur reminded her, "I'm undefeated, remember?"

"You hungry?"

"No, I ate—say, you gonna be home tomorrow night, Ma?"

"I think so."

"Good, because I got a friend coming over for a cooking lesson."

His mother stared at him. "A friend?"

"Yeah."

"From the gym?"

Arthur nodded. "Another fighter."

The Hitchhiker

B y dusk, Ben knew he was north of Birmingham, past the towers that circled the city like a crown of gray stone. It would be near impossible to get a lift at night. People only noticed him at the last minute, with no time to make a decision.

He had never been such a long way. Thumbing lifts between villages back home, he had only to wait ten minutes before a tractor, or someone he knew from school, stopped for him to clamber inside.

He was hundreds of miles from Devon now. Spring had begun with a few warm days. The air smelled of tall weeds.

If nobody picked him up by nightfall, Ben's plan was to crawl behind a row of trees, unroll the sleeping bag from his rucksack, then get inside and lie there until dawn caught him in its net. He would have to stay low, beyond the sweep of headlights. In the morning, he was certain there would be lorries, freshly laden, grinding upward to Manchester and the far north.

He had some money to eat, but not enough for a hotel or

train fare to Scotland—where he'd been promised work with other people his age.

Soon it was completely dark. Ben wondered if he might see a prostitute, or if people might think he was one. Then a car appeared. He raised his arm, standing still so the driver could see his eyes. To his surprise, the vehicle stopped. He hurried toward it, rolling the backpack off his shoulders.

The woman was so tall her seat was pushed all the way back. She had on gym shorts and a sports jacket and was driving the car barefoot.

"I don't normally do this," she said. "But I felt sorry for you." She told him her name was Diane, and that she lived in Walsall and was thirty-four—twice Ben's age.

"Sometimes I drive when I can't sleep," she admitted. "You probably think it's a waste of petrol."

He thought of her bare white thighs, but did not allow himself to look down. Ben said she shouldn't go too far from home. Maybe drop him at the closest junction. But when they approached the first exit, she showed no signs of stopping. Some time later, Diane left the motorway for an unlit slip road. In the distance burned the lights of an all-night petrol station.

"Leave me there if you want," Ben said.

On the forecourt, the car filled with yellow light. Ben could see the woman clearly now. Her hair was dark red and there was a gap between her front teeth.

She unclipped her seat belt, then pulled a pair of flip-flops from the door pocket.

"I'd better fill up."

Ben didn't know if she wanted him to go, or was refueling to drive farther. He got out and stood by the door.

"Think I'll go into the shop," he said. "I'll leave my bag, if that's alright?"

When she lifted her head, Ben glimpsed the outer rim of a birthmark on her neck that she had tried to cover with long hair.

"Don't worry," she told him, "I won't drive off."

A motorcycle policeman in yellow and black stood, like a wasp, stirring coffee in a paper cup. When his radio crackled, he switched it off. In the toilet, people had scribbled and scratched their names on the wall. On his way out, Ben noticed a freezer with pictures of ice creams on the side.

Diane was in the car with the engine running. Ben opened the door and handed her an ice rocket.

"Get in," she said. "I can't drop you here."

They bit their ice rockets without speaking. For early spring it was warm, and Diane had to open a window. An hour passed unnoticed.

"I'm such a loser," she said, after telling Ben about her job in a chain restaurant, "but when I get home, I'm so tired cooking for other people—I just throw something in the microwave."

She grew up in Northampton, but knew Devon as a child when her family had a caravan. She remembered the folding table, damp beds, a small television with its own aerial, birds calling from the trees at dawn, running with her younger brother until suddenly afraid they had gone too far. Fresh cockles from a van; it was as though they were swallowing the sea, she said. Then later on, the thrill of being up late. A bench near the seafront. The weight of chips on her lap; evening unwrapped like a steaming prize.

One day, her father came home from work and said their caravan had been stolen from the storage lot. Thieves must have seen it from the dual carriageway, then gone back at night and forced the gates.

Ben spent his holidays helping on farms, with evenings at the pub. Sometimes they all got drunk and tumbled onto Dartmoor.

When Diane laughed, hair blew in her face. Ben watched her push it away.

Then there was a sign for Blackpool.

"Let's go," Diane said.

"But you're already so far from home."

"C'mon," she said, "it'll be an adventure."

They arrived before two in the morning. Ben was worried about groups of men, drunk and wanting to fight. But the streets were empty, except for a few seagulls who astonished Diane with their size. Many hotels were boarded up, and there were rust marks where letters used to be. Some buildings had lost their roofs, or been blinded by stones thrown from the street. Despite the decay, Diane said there was something about Blackpool that made her happy.

"It was once grand," Ben told her. "During the war."

"Then maybe it's the ghost of other people's happiness I'm feeling," she said, turning onto the seafront.

When they saw the lights of an all-night fish-and-chip shop, Ben said they could get something to eat. The shop was bright and reeked of grease and vinegar. An old man in a white overcoat leaned against a fryer with crossed arms. His hair was cropped short, and his unshaven cheeks drawn in. After salting and peppering the battered fish and steaming chips, he held up a plastic bottle in the shape of a tomato. Ben shook his head.

"Good man," the owner said. "A purist."

Diane had parked near some beach steps. The smell filled the car quickly. They could see Blackpool Tower, and there were some lights—but the main attractions were closed down.

Diane got out and stood barefoot on the pavement. A seagull was in the road, wings snapping as it tried to spill the contents of a paper box. The beach stones were hard to walk on. After choosing a place to sit, Diane said there was a blanket in the car, so Ben went back. He wondered what would happen if he drove away. If she'd be embarrassed to tell the police she had picked up a hitchhiker.

Through the darkness they could hear the sea. Diane took a corner of the blanket and covered her legs. There was only one fish fork in the bag of food—but when Ben handed it to Diane, she speared a chip and gave it back. They could hear the waves and smell salt water.

"I admire you," Diane said. "Just going where you want."

Ben broke open the steaming fish. "It was adventurous of you to pick me up—I could have been anyone."

"Probably not a good idea, right?"

"Except that it was me, and we're here now on the beach eating chips."

The white, scalloped pieces of cod came easily.

"Imagine all the places this fish went," Ben said, "all the things it saw before getting caught."

The meal took a long time to finish because they found there was a lot to tell each other. When Ben thought of a question, he asked it. Any question at all. Nothing seemed silly or personal. He wondered if this was how relationships started. He had kissed several girls, and even an older woman who was drunk at the pub and said she was getting a divorce. But he had never spent all night talking, telling a person things nobody had ever known or cared to ask about.

When there was only skin and hard pieces of batter, the greasy wrapping almost blew away. Diane caught it in midair, then anchored the paper with a few stones.

Ben wondered if he should kiss her now. He tried to imagine what his friends would say—how let down they would be if he did nothing.

But then Diane stood up and they ran down to the water, past shells and bushels of seaweed. The shells glowed white on the sand like magical objects. Diane turned one over with her foot. They could not see much of the ocean, just a dark mass, with the occasional white dot moving along the horizon with shrill gasps. The world felt uninhabited, as though everything they knew and counted on had come to an end.

When they were back on the blanket, Diane stared at him for a long time, and Ben thought something might happen. He pulled a bottle of cider from his jacket.

"This comes from an apple farm near me. A West Country orchard of Pendragons and Crimson Queens. The Pendragons are blood red and the juice comes out pink. It's not very sweet, but makes good cider." Ben looked at the bottle. "I was saving it for a special occasion, but forgot an opener."

Diane took it from him, then pried the cap off with her car key.

"My brother showed me that."

"Then let's toast him," Ben said, as cider foamed out.

Diane raised her arm. "To my brother Andrew."

"To Andy! Wherever he may be tonight."

Ben insisted Diane drink first. It was refreshing after the salty food.

"So where is Andy?"

She passed the bottle back.

"He died," Diane said.

"Bloody hell, I'm sorry."

"A week before his seventeenth birthday. One of the last things he told me was how upset he was about not getting his driving license. There was a nurse he wanted to ask out."

When Diane smiled, Ben saw the gap between her teeth again.

"That was Andy," she said. "Remember when I told you our caravan was stolen?"

Ben nodded.

"Well, it wasn't. My parents sold it to pay for special treatments. But they didn't work. Nothing worked in the end."

Ben looked into the sky. Very dark over the sea where there was no streetlight.

"I still think about where he went." Her voice was shaking now. "Where the dead go."

Ben imagined what it was like after. Forcing themselves to eat. The silence where words and laughter would have been. An emptiness they would learn to carry around.

He tried to picture Diane's face when she was told her brother was dead.

Their caravan would have been long gone by then, full of other voices, other bare feet on the thin carpet, other sleeping bodies under sheets in the curtained light. But in memory it would always be theirs, and never change or grow old, or belong to anyone else.

When everything had been said, she lay down. Ben leaned back on his elbows, and their arms touched. He waited for Diane to move. He wondered if she knew they were touching.

A few hours later Ben opened his eyes and sat up quickly. A wet dog stood with a stick in its mouth. Night was draining into the sea.

When they got back to the car, it was almost six. The eastern sky was dazzling. Gloss white paint on iron benches looked bright and delicate.

They talked a little but were mostly silent. Ben noticed she'd kept the fish fork. It was under the hand brake with some coins and the wrapper from her ice rocket.

When they came to a busy roundabout, Ben said it was probably the best place to get out. It was the morning of a different day. The roads were full of people going to work. Children drifting in groups toward school fields.

Diane pulled over and slipped some notes from her wallet.

"Take the train the rest of the way."

Ben looked at the money in her hands.

"Please," she said. "Take something for your journey."

When he closed the door, they stared at one another through the glass, but only her outline was visible. It was the first of many times he would try to remember her face, the first of many times he would look for someone and not see them— search for someone whose absence defined him.

Not Dying

The Art of Fugue

"An Incomplete Work of Unspecified Instrumentation"

A piece in which the voices come in,
And the listeners go out, one by one.

—SAINT-SAËNS

Author's Note

When I was in Kentucky, one of my neighbors lived alone and never had visitors. His speech was extremely delayed and he always wore the same thing—denim overalls with a dozen key chains dangling from a belt loop. My favorite was a doll's shoe in the form of an ice skate. He worked somewhere local, but I don't know where. And he walked slowly, taking small steps.

Sometimes I would hear his TV through the wall. But sometimes it was him, talking on the telephone.

He would disappear on weekends and holidays; I thought he was with his parents, but I later learned he had a wife and a daughter in the northern part of the state.

One night, we came to our respective doors at the same time.

"I wasn't always like this," he said.

A week later it happened again. But this time he invited me in. On the table was a bowl of nuts with chocolate pieces mixed in. On the wall, framed pictures of a woman and a teenage girl in a wheelchair. He said the child was his daughter.

The following story is inspired by what he told me over the next five hours.

1.

For a long time all he could do was lie still with his eyes closed.

It was snowing then.

Flakes tumbled from the sky and broke apart on the windshield. The truck was stiff because the engine had been off since dark.

2.

The radio was on, but low. When a powerful voice rose in anger to announce the end of the world, Lenny sat up. The voice wanted listeners to know it loved them. But most of all it was God's love that mattered. Then the voice went silent with the snow all around still falling.

Lenny's wife and daughter were inside the house. He could see their faces in his mind, but could not hold their faces steady. They flickered and broke apart as though memory were another trick of light on water.

He turned the radio dial. Went from one end to the other, but caught not one sentence, nor one word, nor a single note of music. All had gone quiet. He reached for a plastic-wrapped soft pack of cigarettes. They were deep in the glove box where his wife or daughter wouldn't find them when foraging for candies. He struck a paper match, then watched blue smoke curl through a crack in the window.

After smoking, Lenny flicked out the glowing end and lay on his back across the bench seat of the old Ford pickup. Then he closed his eyes with radio static all around and cold seeping in through his heavy coat.

3.

Repent, the voice had said. *The end is near.*

Lenny tried to imagine what it would be like. The voice said sometime tomorrow, early or late it didn't know—but in a few hours the Earth would no longer exist. Even in memory.

Lenny watched the snow falling. Then pictured himself alongside his wife and ten-year-old daughter in the master bedroom of the farmhouse they had rented for the weekend.

The idea had been to get away from the city.

A vacation house in the mountains. Hours from anywhere, with no television, Internet, or cell phone reception. A weekend of long meals, building fires, talking—Monopoly.

If the end of the world were coming, Lenny thought, we'd be better off in the country. He was calm because he didn't believe it. He tried to imagine what the city would be like: a screaming crowd going madly in all directions; fire; shoes and flattened pieces of clothing on the road; barricades of upside-down shopping carts; people getting pulled from their vehicles.

If it happened tomorrow as the voice had said, they would die quietly in a house that was not their home. Most likely upstairs in the yellow bedroom, with their daughter between them.

Jane's doll too, in sweater and ice skates.

4.

Lenny tried to imagine how dying would feel. He closed his eyes and let his head hang to one side. Stopped his breathing.

But his mind was fixed on the idea of escape. Getting Carolin and Jane to safety. Somewhere far away, a cliff overlooking plains, faces streaked with dirt, they sob at lines of smoke in the distance; the smoldering remains of a lost race.

The heat of fire carried him back to childhood. A Western Shoshone reservation in Nevada.

Outside the trailer, scattered toys, a washing machine full of empty bottles, the neighbor's '71 Chevy Cheyenne with flat tires and faded paint.

Low, blowing, pale-green desert grass all around.

Lenny used to sit watching the long road up the mountain for a cloud. Somebody coming or somebody gone. He wanted to be outside when the cloud was his father. To show he'd been waiting. That he was loyal like the men in westerns.

He knew there was a world beyond the sun-red dust and always blowing wind. He'd seen people on television in gray cities of falling rain.

He knew the sea from books. On the page it didn't move; still, the oceans and tides conjured from his weekly bath were enough to flood the world.

When Lenny was ten, his mother took him on their first

vacation. A noiseless cloud rolling down the mountain with no one watching. Two people in a white car with soda, chips, and borrowed Nevada plates. A mother and son leaving the reservation for a body of water in Arizona, where Lenny would once again be weightless.

5.

If the world *were* ending he would try and get his girls to the desert. It was ground that remembered him. Perhaps there would be other survivors who knew more and had a plan?

Would they believe they'd been spared for a reason? That they were special? That's how religion is born, Lenny figured, still lying there on his back in the truck. And that's why the voice was so passionate. Religion preys on the weak. It is born through fear. To be saved you must give up hope in anything else. Freedom through servitude. Then you'll be ready. For Him.

Lenny laughed because his wife would have said *Her*. But if there was anything, he thought—it had to be nothing like us, no blood, nor flesh, not even a face.

Outside it was still coming down, like the bones of all those who had come before.

Lenny's daughter, Jane, was *delivered* in a city called Albany, at a hospital of redbrick and glass. He hesitated to say *born*, feeling now, lying there in the cold, that bodies do not create life, but channel it.

Then he lit another cigarette and smoked until it was hot in his fingers.

6.

Lenny felt he should do something. Maybe drive to a gas station or find a town. He could know then. There would be lights on and people outside their homes.

He sat up and tried the radio dial again, his mind rolling along with the static. Anticipation like a net. The announcer must have been a fanatic, going through a nervous breakdown, or angry at being fired and attempting to spread fear in his last moments on the air.

Lenny's body craved a lick of bourbon, or a finger of brandy in a heavy glass. Something to get in his gums. He'd been sober for almost a decade—since becoming engaged to Carolin. But smoking was a different matter. He liked one every night at exactly the same time. If Jane and Carolin were sleeping he'd have another. Then, if he was up late, a third.

It was soon past midnight.

He sat up and opened the door of the truck slowly, then took a few steps outside. It didn't feel like the world was ending. Just another long winter's night. But he was careful to close the truck door with only a click. His lips were sticking and tasted of blood.

The sky had cleared for a moment, and he stared up into the bowl of stars. Set loose his breath. Seeing it reminded him of ancestors praying to the souls of dying animals. Made him wonder if it was possible to live without eyes and a mouth, a brain and limbs, blood and hair.

7.

Part of him wanted to get back in the truck and just drive—make sure there was nothing in what he'd heard on the radio. He could surely leave the girls for an hour. Find a diner—get fried eggs and black coffee.

When he was in high school, there was a place he went to. It wasn't far from the reservation where he lived with his mother. An hour west. Deep in the desert. It was open all night, served hamburgers and onion rings. A lottery machine on the counter. Popular with Native Americans, but veterans too. A place to *go* drunk. A home for those who found no rest in sleep.

Summer nights were baking hot. Lenny used to stand outside, listening to the desert and the grind of diesel trucks making time out of Reno.

Sometimes he got drunk and slept in the car with the windows open.

Lenny knew a lot of people in that place and had good friends on the rez. But after high school, he took off for Arizona. To live near the lake he'd loved as a boy.

8.

Years passed. It was exciting to live away from home. The black cowboy hat his mother gave him as a graduation present was dusty and worn out. He called her once a week and sometimes she visited.

One Saturday, after ripping up an old fence for his neighbor, Lenny drove to the lake with the intention of cooling off.

There was a young woman on the beach staring at the water with her knees up. A blue swimsuit matched her eyes. She moved her fingers in the sand like she was drawing. One of her friends was getting buried.

Lenny did not feel love when he saw her, just disappointment at how they would never meet. He wondered if other people felt things for strangers, then carried the weight of that absence.

There was no wind that day. People just stood in the water. Some were playing games in the water, but Lenny was just standing in it, trying to cool off.

8.1.

He couldn't believe it later on in the parking lot. She had a flat tire, and there was no one else around. They had chosen to go home at the same moment. He reached into his truck for the black cowboy hat, then went back.

"Looks like you've got a flat there, miss."

"Darn it!" she said, looking around. "And my friends are gone."

Lenny could see the outline of her bathing suit under a loose T-shirt, but kept his eyes on the tire.

"You probably went over a nail."

"Will that do it?"

"A nail? Sure." Lenny couldn't believe how she didn't know the power she had over others.

"I can put the spare on for you?" he offered.

"I think I'll be okay."

Lenny stared at how sunk down the car looked with the crushed tire.

"I wouldn't want to keep you," she said quickly. "It's probably a lot of trouble, right?"

"It's no trouble. I could change tires all day."

"Are you a mechanic?"

He shook his head. "Just like fixing things."

"You'd get along with my dad then. He was a cop, but now he works on old cars."

"What kind?"
"Ford trucks, mostly."
"No kidding?"

8.2.

When they looked in the trunk there was no spare. Lenny had to drive her home. She didn't seem nervous, but he tried to think of things that would make her feel safe.

"I'll fix that tire for you tomorrow."

"You don't have to."

"I'll go to a junkyard in Boulder City, get you a wheel. Then we'll drive out to the beach and put it on."

"You can't do that."

"It's no problem."

"Don't you have things to do? It's Sunday."

Lenny laughed. "Like church?"

"Well I don't know . . . do you think it'll cost a lot?"

"I don't think it will. A wheel like that. Can't be more than fourteen inches. Hopefully the junkyard wheel will have a good tire already on it."

"I'm Carolin," she said, turning her body to face him.

"You're not from Arizona, I can tell."

"How can you tell?" she said.

"Your accent, I guess."

"I'm from Albany."

"Where's that?"

"New York."

"Wow, city girl."

This made her laugh. Lenny looked at the road. He couldn't believe the girl from the beach was in his truck.

8.3.

They rode out to a junkyard in Boulder City the next day, but it was closed, so Lenny bought something from the auto shop to spray in the tire and make it hard. He followed her from the lake with his hazard lights blinking all the way to her house.

That night they had Mexican food on the patio. She went barefoot. Lenny saw she had painted her toes. After eating, she brought him inside to watch television. They laughed along with the people they couldn't see. She said he could stay, then took him into her room. Streetlight lit up her bed. They kissed and she undressed with the windows open, insects rattling in the trees.

A few days later they met to play minigolf and eat something. After eating, it felt early so they drove a long way to the college she had in mind. The parking lot was empty but for Lenny's truck. He could see his red taillights in the rearview mirror. Carolin was saving up for the tuition payments, and getting her state residency.

The neighbors soon got used to seeing a Ford pickup parked outside her yellow house. Some had things they needed doing and trusted Lenny, because at first he wouldn't take money. His truck was white with a bench seat. The bumpers were rusted. One end was twisted out. Carolin said he should save money too. Then buy a garage and fix up old cars, like her dad.

Sometimes Lenny drove her to the sacred grounds. He had a blow-up mattress in the back and they used it on clear nights when the stars were more powerful than anything they had seen on Earth. It felt good to talk like that, without being afraid, as though being together meant taming things from the past.

Lenny even told her about his father disappearing; about when that had happened to him and his mother back in Nevada.

9.

A year after they met, Carolin had to go back east because her father got cancer. They sold her small car and piled their belongings in the back of Lenny's truck under a blue tarp.

That was many years ago. But Lenny knew the story of how he met Carolin would one day be thousands of years old. One day millions. Not lost, but lodged somewhere in the darkness between stars, waiting to be reclaimed. The certainty that all happiness would be forgotten made Lenny value it more. But he also sensed a deeper happiness. One that was unexpected, that came later, without pain and the memory of others.

He couldn't see any stars now from the driveway, but knew they were somewhere through the freezing air, beyond the snow and the clouds, beyond the mountains, far away.

He hoped he might feel better in the house. Shake off the radio announcer's words like snow from his jacket. Perhaps convince himself it was a joke or he'd misheard—or was caught in some complicated dream where you wake up, but in truth you've gone deeper. Inside the farmhouse, the fire he'd lit with his daughter was still going. He would tell her in the morning what a good job she had done. He sat on the carpet in his socks. Could feel the heat pushing his face.

Jane and Carolin were sleeping upstairs. He thought he might go and look at them. Listen to them breathe.

When they woke in seven or eight hours, the sky would be a low flare of orange beyond the dumb, packed snow.

Jane would want to go outside and play. She had been born in Albany and was used to the winters. Carolin would come downstairs with her book, wearing glasses, looking for coffee and toast. That was what tomorrow would be like, unless Lenny woke his wife to repeat what he'd heard in the truck.

Carolin would listen with her eyes closed. Groan and turn over.

Come to bed now, she would say.

You're just scared because we hit that ice driving up here.

But we're fine, Lenny—we're okay.

Nothing happened.

10.

He sat there facing the flames his daughter had summoned. Transfixed by thought and by heat. At least they would be together. He felt they were together, even after familiarity had culled the anxiety mistaken for love.

But of course, nothing was going to happen. He would soon tramp upstairs and fall asleep, let the world disappear but not end. He would remember the announcer's voice, but it would have no power over him. Words are the shadows of things—not the things themselves.

11.

Lenny would have known if such an event were even a possibility. Scientists would have taken over the television and told everyone months ago. He would not have driven into the mountains for the weekend, for snowshoeing, hot chocolate, and Monopoly. How Jane loved it when Lenny went to jail.

But there was no doubt in the announcer's voice. He believed it himself for sure. How do people like that get on the air? Lenny thought. How are they allowed?

He felt anger then. How people could mistake conviction for truth. Maybe there were others who actually accepted what this man was saying? What if there were people out there now, killing themselves to escape death?

Such thoughts made Lenny realize how tired he was. Made him feel like going upstairs to Carolin and Jane.

He got up off the living room floor and went to the kitchen to make hot chocolate. Jane had brought a box of packets. It was probably just radio drama, or a religious show—fire and brimstone every week—with a telephone number for donations. And of course it was late, and Lenny was aware his mind might be playing tricks. His unease most likely the result of jumbled-up feelings from their harrowing car journey up the mountain. They had skidded to the side of the road after seeing a bright light, a blinding light that came toward them.

Standing over the kettle, Lenny warmed his hands on

the steam. What would he do if something really were taking place?

When he was alone, he sometimes had fantasies. He would pretend something was going on—a car accident; earthquake; things on fire—then picture Carolin on his back, Jane in his arms.

In real life, Lenny knew if the world were ending, saving his family would be a matter of chance rather than courage. He'd owned a gun out west, but then he met Carolin and she didn't like guns and, to be honest, he couldn't shoot anyway.

As he poured boiling water onto the heap of brown powder, hard white pieces floated to the top and transformed into marshmallows. They reminded Lenny of Jane's baby teeth.

The preacher on the radio had said total devastation with no escape. *Gather your loved ones*, he had said, *for the day of reckoning is here.*

Lenny imagined rocking them awake. Telling Jane to put on her slippers and come downstairs, there is something important to tell. As he thought of doing this, he carried his hot chocolate to the living room and looked around, deciding where they would sit when he told them. The fire going strong, it would flicker on the surface of their eyes.

Maybe they should eat something before he tells them? Maybe if they ate, it would be better?

He knew what Jane would want and imagined preparing a last meal. The onion so white. He would break the pasta and add salt to quicken the boil. He would think: This is our last meal. They would all die with the food in their stomachs. Lenny wondered if most people died with food in their stomachs.

He imagined his daughter Jane as an old lady with her parents long gone. Pictured her in a nursing home trembling on the couch with no one alive who knew or remembered her. There were people like that everywhere, who had outlived their lives.

The thought of it made Lenny want to rush upstairs. Until hearing the preacher's words, he hadn't fully understood how one day they would be separated.

The world might not end, but they would. And *that* was the forever part. Not love.

Love was just something tiny and bright with eternity on all sides.

12.

When the fire was just a deep, rolling glow, Lenny went into the hall. It was cold near the front door of the farmhouse. He peered through the darkness up the staircase. Maybe he should see what was happening. It was almost two in the morning. He had been on the couch for a long time.

The announcer had said bright light followed by judgment.

But the worst . . . Lenny thought . . . the absolute worst, would not be telling them the end was coming—or even the dying. The worst would be after that, when they were gone—lost from one another with no hope of ever meeting again.

Jane was only ten years old and might be afraid if she were alone. Without memory, she might not realize there had once been two people called Lenny and Carolin, who created her body, then put food in her mouth, changed her diapers, bathed her in the sink of a pink house in Albany, read stories, lied about animals being able to talk, and wrote messages on cards once a year to make her feel important.

Lenny heard the announcer's voice speaking to him directly—but now it was more like the voice of his father, an oilman who his mother said used to walk around with a diamond-tipped drill bit in a briefcase. Lenny met him once. But he wasn't carrying a briefcase, just a bottle.

Lenny went back in the living room. Tried anchoring himself to reality by staring at his empty mug. Then the mantelpiece; the glowing logs he and Jane had piled into the grate; a painting of the house they were in. He stood and went closer. Wondered if *inside* the painting of the house there was a painting of the house.

He considered that he was already dead. And there was really no one upstairs. No upstairs even, and he was imagining everything to get through this part of the dying process. On the other side of the curtain, where the living dwell, it was summer. Carolin and Jane were back home in Albany going on with their lives and having lunch, or picking out shoes online, or in bed watching television—learning to live without him, happiness leaking back into their lives.

He could rest then. If he knew Jane and Carolin could be happy without him, dying wouldn't be so bad after all. And as a father and a husband, it might be nice to go on ahead. Soften the unknown. Get everything ready. Be waiting with his arms out.

13.

Hours before, when they were packing up the car to escape Albany for the weekend, Lenny noticed his daughter just standing there in the house. She would be eleven soon, and no longer believed in the tooth fairy or Santa Claus. Jane wanted to be older, and was waiting for it to happen the way some people wait for an inheritance.

Carolin had taken her shopping the weekend before to pick out bras. There was probably a small bra in the room upstairs where she was sleeping right at this minute. Lenny loved seeing Jane's shoes everywhere at home, and staring into the yard at her toys full of rain.

Training bras, Carolin had said, help girls prepare mentally for the coming change. But Jane wasn't wearing one when Lenny saw her standing there in the hall that morning as they packed for the trip. He could tell she wasn't wearing one—and was going to ask if she should, but then felt it was wrong of him to have noticed.

Every time he got used to a new Jane, she would change again. At times, it was as though a stranger had taken over her body, making her say and do things that his old daughter would never have said or done.

Loading up the truck, the air smelled like wood smoke, pine, and diesel. With the front door open, cold went through the house like a broom. Lenny knew it was going to snow pretty bad, and tied a blue tarp over their suitcases. The same tarp he'd used years before, moving east with Carolin to watch her father die.

14.

Lenny went back to the kitchen. Set his cup in the sink.

Then he opened the refrigerator door and stood there, stuffing coconut pie into his mouth. Carolin had brought some from the diner where they stopped to eat.

Then he went back to the fire. Red coals were now breaking apart. He put a log on. One of them was covered in green lichen. It would be a while before the fresh wood took flame, but the heat from the cinders was steady.

Tomorrow, he planned on taking the girls hiking deep in the woods. Jane was worried about bears, but Carolin said they would most likely be hibernating.

Lenny imagined a bear loping toward them. If Carolin were caught first, he'd put Jane down and fight to save his wife. He imagined flesh coming off in strips, then his hand in the bear's stomach. The stump shooting blood. Carolin's scarf as a tourniquet. Jane still holding her doll with its ice skates on. If only the blades were real.

If there had been an Internet connection in the farmhouse, Lenny would have looked up bear attacks. Was it safe to carry Hershey's Kisses in your pocket? Was chocolate to bears like blood to sharks? What if Carolin was menstruating? Lenny thought quickly. Then he realized it was honey, not chocolate or blood, that bears like. He knew that from Jane's book *Winnie the Pooh*.

If the world came to an end as the man on the radio said,

Jane would never menstruate. According to nature, her body would have been meaningless. Jane's life, meaningless. Lenny just couldn't imagine it.

But what did the opinion of one religious fanatic matter?

Out west they were everywhere, screaming and hollering, standing by the road toting signs and eyeballing truckers. One of them must have wandered onto the radio. That's all it was.

As a child he'd tried to believe in God more than anything. If his missing father *was* dead, Lenny wanted him to be in heaven. And if he wasn't? Maybe God would guide him home. But in the end, it's hard to believe in something you can't feel.

There were so many things he couldn't understand.

For instance, heaven. Didn't people there watch their loved ones suffering on Earth without them? How could they be happy seeing that? And if heaven dwellers didn't know about people suffering on Earth because they left their memories behind in their bodies—how would they know who to reunite with later?

Hell was worse.

Lenny figured that if his father had gone to hell, he might as well go there too, at least to get some answers. It would have been torture to know his dad was in hell if he himself ended up in heaven. In that case heaven would be hell for him. But if his daddy were in heaven, and he, Lenny, eventually went to hell for the few bad things he'd done—then it would be okay, because he'd know his father and mother were safe. So hell would be heaven because he wouldn't have to worry. More important than that—what if he lied and said he believed in God when deep down he didn't? Then it was all for nothing anyway—as God would know he had been lying.

When he was in high school he tried to get answers from his teachers. But nobody knew anything, as though what they hadn't thought of didn't exist.

Driving up the mountain they saw a tractor-trailer with JESUS IS LORD on the back. Jane asked what it meant, but Lenny still didn't know.

15.

When they arrived at the house, Lenny helped unpack Jane's clothes. There was an old chest of drawers in her room that had been painted over several times. *Wood is living*, he'd told her. *It has a spirit*. His daughter sat watching her father take things out and fold them.

Lenny could tell she was thinking things but not saying them. That happened more and more now she was older. Though she still played with toys. Lenny listened sometimes through her bedroom door. To the animal voices. To the dolls being moved around in their made-up lives.

16.

That was earlier when they arrived, a matter of several hours, but to Lenny another lifetime. They had stopped for dinner on the way up because of snow. The roads had gotten worse and worse. Cars abandoned at strange angles. Carolin usually slept on long journeys, but was too afraid this time. She felt better when they stopped to eat. After that she closed her eyes.

Finding the house they had rented was easy because there were no other cars. They could crawl along and read the numbers on mailboxes. Lenny didn't want to leave them alone in the truck, and so they went up the steps to the dark house together. When Lenny got the door open, Jane screamed there was someone in the house, but it was just Lenny's reflection in a hall mirror.

It was late and they were excited to be away from home. Carolin went upstairs, and Lenny took Jane outside to explore the barn. The driveway was ice with some fresh powder. When they came back in, they thought Carolin was unpacking, but when they went upstairs she was asleep in her clothes on a patchwork comforter. Their laughing woke her up.

An hour later, when Carolin went to bed for real, Lenny let Jane stay up and help build the fire. After brushing teeth, they sat on the couch. She wanted to play Monopoly. But it was too late for Monopoly. That game took a long time.

When Lenny said no, she cried, which meant she was tired. For a while they just sat there, not playing Monopoly.

"So how's school?"

"Good."

"What's your favorite class?"

"Recess."

Then the room got hot because the fire was really going. They could hear it crackling, as though trying to tell them things.

After a while Jane leaned into her father.

"The logs look like elephant legs, Dad."

"Yeah."

"Fire is weird. I mean, where does it come from?"

"I don't know, except what I learned at the reservation school when I was a boy."

"Tell me."

"Well, I guess the story goes that after people and animals got made, there was a rattlesnake who was popular with everybody, because they liked the sound of his rattle. So they kept bothering him and he couldn't get no sleep for being poked. So he went to an elder and told him, and the elder took a hair from his own face and cut it into little bits, which made teeth for the rattlesnake's mouth. *If anyone comes near you again*, the elder said, *you just bite them*. A bit later a rabbit went to the rattlesnake and poked him to hear the rattle, so Rattlesnake bit him, and Rabbit was mad and scratched Rattlesnake and got bit again. And then Rabbit got sick from the bites and died."

"The rabbit died?" Jane said. "That's sad."

"Yeah, and no one had ever died before, and the people and animals didn't know what to do. If they buried Rabbit, Coyote would dig him up. If they put him in a tree, Coyote would find him there too. So at last they decided to burn him. But there was no fire on the Earth yet, so the animals and people sent Coyote on a long journey to get some from Sun. But Coyote thought he was being tricked and kept stopping to look back."

"What happened then?"

"While Coyote was gone, another animal figured out how to make fire by twirling a stick onto another stick, and when Coyote saw smoke in the sky, he rushed home. But the animals had formed a circle around the fire, so Coyote ran around the circle, until he found two short animals to jump over, and then he dove into the fire, where he tried to get Rabbit's heart but burned his tongue, which is still red to this day."

"Is that story true?"

"I don't know."

"Coyotes do have red tongues so it must be, right?"

"Yeah, it must be."

Jane and her father looked into the flames, at Rabbit's glowing heart.

"You know," Lenny said, "when I was your age, I felt sorry for Coyote because the other animals didn't want him."

Jane nodded. "I thought that too. Daddy, can I ask you something?"

"You can ask me anything."

"Can we play Monopoly?"

. . .

Upstairs, she wanted another story, but her eyes were closing. Lenny knew she was sleeping when her face lost its expression. He wondered where she was then. If she knew her father was watching from outside the darkness, beyond the thump of her own fiery heart, in the quiet flames of sleep.

17.

Just before three, Lenny was exploring the farmhouse when he came upon something that frightened him.

There was no truth in what he'd heard on the radio. He knew that. But when he noticed the newspapers and the magazines, he decided, right then and there, to go on a quick journey into the woods on foot, to try and pick up reception on his cell phone.

His boots were by the door beneath a heavy coat that was stuffed with a hat and tan gloves, Christmas presents from Carolin's mother. In winter he rubbed his boots and Jane's boots with mink oil. He could smell it now as he pulled them on. He tried to go out quietly, but the screen door yawned before snapping shut.

At first he did not feel the cold except on the surface of his cheeks.

Beyond the driveway, snow was waist high. How deep it would get, he didn't know. Carolin lost reception on her phone an hour before they arrived at the house—but going higher might bring it back.

He turned his hips through the white powder. Clambered over roots and mounds of frozen earth. The temperature was too low for the snow on his clothes to melt. It covered him like powdered sugar. He moved through the cold wilderness like his ancestors.

If Lenny hadn't found those magazines on the table by

the fire, he might have just gone up to bed. Of course, he knew the easiest thing would have been to drive somewhere, but starting the truck would have woken Carolin—pulled her to the window in time to see the glow of taillights. He would have had to explain when he got back, and she'd laugh or get annoyed.

If he could get a single bar for a few seconds, he would know. He could check the television or a news website and be satisfied then. He could go back inside, peel off his clothes, and get into bed with his wife. He did not wish to return without a feeling of certainty, and kept moving through the dark, clustered trees, entering first with fear, then with his body.

When the snow shallowed, dead branches made it easy to trip. The ground was rocky and the wind whipped fiercely at his bare cheeks. Lenny worried it would blow snow over his tracks. He tried to reassure himself that while he might be lost, the trees were not; the owls were not; the moon was home.

He stopped and took out his phone to check for service. The screen was a moist pattern of sweat. He didn't want to climb anymore. The summit was farther than he'd imagined, and the cold was inside his clothes. Lenny knew he had to be careful. Bodies were sometimes discovered in early spring by hikers—the result of a wrong step.

Lenny did not want to die and remembered driving upstate that night with Carolin and Jane beside him on the bench seat of the Ford. How good it felt with their bodies touching.

He stood tall now and held the device at arm's length

toward the moon. It was too far from his face to check, so he just held it there, waving slightly as though trying to get the attention of something in the sky.

All because he'd seen articles in those magazines. That was why reassurance was necessary. Lucky he and Jane hadn't used them for the fire or else he'd never know.

When he brought the device back to his face, he could see that nothing had changed. Not a single bar of service. Lenny felt foolish suddenly, as though he was a child with no sense of the things that were possible and impossible.

Carolin would laugh when he told her how afraid he had been. Jane would have wanted to come. He would recount the story over black coffee and toast.

At some point on the way down his phone vibrated. He grabbed at it, clumsily pulling the device from his pocket. No bars, but a single text message from Carolin's mother in Albany. A line of words. Some proof that life was taking place as normal beyond the mountain.

But when Lenny read it, there was not the flood of relief he had anticipated. So he read it again. Then over and over, even saying the words out loud, not moving an inch until he could grasp the meaning. He even considered each word on its own without the others, to see if that changed anything.

He began to feel weakness in his hands and feet. It was something he'd first experienced as a little boy, when his mother got beaten on the steps of their trailer by people she owed money to.

18.

It was peaceful the rest of the way. He tried to keep his worry at a distance, at least until he was in the house again. When the woods leveled off, the snow deepened, and Lenny found the trail he had made, a valley of ruffled white. He stopped to look at the phone. His face took on the glow of the screen as he moved, a small traveler, along the path of a single sentence. She could have meant something else, he thought. Her phone might have changed the words to what it thought she should say. That happened all the time.

When Lenny found the mouth of the driveway, there was his gleaming truck. He remembered Jane's gloved hand on the fender earlier. Her voice counting down. Then holding hands as they ran across fresh snow onto a patch of bare ice, sliding effortlessly in their shoes.

As he stood there in the very cold night, it occurred to Lenny that the world had many *good* things.

It didn't have to have anything good, but it did.

And he had felt them.

19.

Once inside the house, Lenny locked himself in the downstairs toilet and stripped to his underwear. With the light off, it felt even more like a dream and all he had to do was keep going until it was possible to wake up. The porcelain toilet seat was freezing. He could smell disinfectant from a plastic bottle on the tile floor.

He felt such a strong desire to go upstairs and wake his family—but what would they think, seeing him like this?

It was more than just the radio announcer's voice now. It was the information he'd discovered in the magazines, and the text message.

He padded barefoot to the living room and stood shivering before the fire.

As much as he wanted to rip out and burn the articles he had found, they were physical proof that he wasn't going crazy—that this wasn't some kind of psychotic episode. The articles had been written and printed, without anyone knowing there was someone called Lenny from Nevada sitting in a Ford truck smoking with the radio on.

For a while he just walked around the house in his underwear, tidying up and looking through any window for the lights of a passing vehicle. If people were out driving, then it was definitely not real. Unless they were driving a certain way. Like trying to escape.

When the fire waned, he threw on fresh logs. Then he

sat and waited for the wood to flame, letting heat from the coals spread over his bare chest and arms.

On the top of a neat pile next to his phone was the *American Geographic* magazine, dated two months back, with cover illustration of a blue planet colliding with the sun. In the pictures, the world looked small and insignificant. Inside there was a drawing of the sun's fire reflected on the Earth's watery surface—the way a human eye sometimes takes on a version of what it sees.

A Trillion-to-One Chance of Helio-Eradication, Experts Say, but the Risk Is There . . .

At an impromptu conference in Geneva last month, scientists from the Brisbane Space Alliance, New Brunswick Observatory, London's Greenwich Hub, and the Chinese People's Party Institute for the Cosmos met to discuss the Earth's recent change in orbit . . .

Underneath, Lenny had placed a copy of the *New York Sun*, where the idea had been front-page news a month before:

Scientists in Chile Fear Hot End

Despite calls by government officials in Santiago for calm, and measures for information containment, several of Chile's leading space experts have put forward their fear that the Earth is heading for destruction. Although Western cosmologists say this is a remote possibility, they agree that global warming has heated the planet so significantly, a change in the Earth's orbit may be inevitable.

20.

Lenny went to the kitchen again. He was shivering and starting to panic. If it were true, then his responsibility now would be to spare them unimaginable suffering—not seek comfort for himself by telling them.

He imagined himself with a pillow. Hovering as they slept. Arms might not be enough—he would have to press with his whole body. There might be a struggle, legs kicking, arms flailing—Jane's small torso writhing under his grip like a pinned snake. But it was the lesser of two evils, as his mother might have said.

Breathing would cease in less than a minute. The brain is starved. The heart stops. Blood is still. Hours before the collective eye of mankind closes in pain and terror.

It must have happened before, Lenny thought, when the certainty of a painful death was known. The Second World War. Those camps where Jews were sent to be murdered, one by one, mother by mother, father by father, daughter by daughter, son by son. Every heart had belonged to someone, somewhere.

Lenny had seen films about it, but there were those who were actually present, those whose cries tore the air, whose bones are in earth, turning every thousand years. Those whose lives we still touch through the sadness of beautiful things.

21.

It reminded Lenny of a story from the Bible he'd heard in school on the reservation. About a king who sent soldiers to kill every male child under the age of two. Right in front of their parents and siblings, the soldiers just ripped open the small bodies with swords.

Lenny wondered how it would feel to see Carolin's body after he'd done it. If he would hold her close or if he would feel nothing. She'd have to be first, for if she woke up while he was standing over Jane, she would attack him.

Once he explained, she would understand. They would sit down beside Jane's body, knowing they had done their best as parents.

Jane had always been a heavy sleeper, but if she did wake up while Lenny was going at it with her mother, he could pretend she had a fever and he was trying some new treatment on her, pillow therapy. They might even laugh about it.

Jane was so young. She would never get to have a first kiss. Her greatest love would have been for her parents and her doll.

Lenny remembered the first time he saw his daughter frightened for her life. It was in Pennsylvania a few years back when the roller coaster they were on suddenly stopped while they were upside down. Jane forced herself to laugh at first . . . thought it was part of the ride. But then there were people below running. Cars with flashing lights. Lenny tried to keep her calm, said to open her knees and wedge herself inside the car. If the bar released he wanted her to have a chance. He was heavy and would plummet like a stone. He got the belt from around his pants to tie her in—but she was getting in such a state he had to shout at her.

He found out later they were trapped for fifty-seven seconds. Not quite a minute, yet for Jane it was a major part of her childhood, something by which she would judge all future incidents of fear.

For the last twenty seconds of being trapped, some of the other people were really screaming. *Please, God! I love you, my Lord!*

The truth was almost too simple to grasp.

A tree limb had fallen on the track ahead. The girl working the controls saw it on her monitor and pressed the emergency stop. People were in a panic, Lenny thought, when the truth was they were being saved by an unseen hand.

An hour later the ride was running again. Lenny, Jane, and Carolin watched it from a bench, eating free ice cream, listening to the screams.

In the kitchen, Lenny turned the faucet and cupped his hands. The water was warm and went easily down his throat. The kitchen must have been where the original family spent their time. There was no table now, but the floor was marked where the legs had been. Back home in Albany, in their pink house on Calyer Street, there was a table where Jane did her homework. Once a week they watched a film and ate dinner on the couch. Going over his life now, there were things he wished he had done differently.

Times when he could have been kinder.

Last week, when Jane got up from the couch she knocked over her glass of lemonade.

"Why are you so clumsy?" he had said.

Carolin wasn't home from work yet.

Jane just stood there, looking at the watery hand on the floor.

"Get some paper towels, Jane. It's your mess, so clean it."

He could see she wanted to cry, but it didn't matter to him then.

"How old are you?"

She didn't answer. He tried to stop himself.

"Almost eleven, Jane, and you can't have a glass of lemonade without disaster?"

He wanted it to sound like an observation. But he knew, deep down, it wasn't an observation—but fear of his own failure. And how that brought them closer to death.

Then Jane was on the floor wiping up the spill. After she had cleaned up the lemonade she ran to her room but was sobbing before she got there.

"Aren't you going to finish watching the movie?" he shouted.

Lenny looked across the dark farmhouse kitchen toward the silverware drawer. Imagined taking a knife and driving it into his stomach.

Why did he make his daughter cry?

He wanted to rush upstairs now and wake her. Beg forgiveness. But she had already forgiven him. Because she was a child.

Lenny imagined carrying their bodies into the snow after. The cold might preserve how they had looked to him in life. He would brush the hair from their faces.

Lenny got up and rushed to the foot of the stairs. Cold air near the front door stung his bare skin. On the mat were Jane's Doc Marten boots. They'd bought them on a trip to New England. Jane had wanted a pair for months. Lenny remembered seeing her walk out of the shop with her old shoes in a box. That was last year. She cut her hair then too. It used to be long, but she wanted it short because of a singer she liked.

When they arrived at the house several hours ago, Carolin said it must have belonged to a farm family. Lenny imagined horses outside waiting to be stabled and fed.

After getting their things from under the blue tarp, Carolin went upstairs. Lenny and Jane still had their coats on and went out to look at the barn. Once they had kicked away enough snow to get the door open, they went in. It smelled of cold water and rust. They saw children's bicycles stacked against one another, with flat tires and cobwebs in the wheels. Jane wanted to know where the children were now, where they had gone without their bikes.

22.

Then suddenly, Lenny fell to his knees with a gasp of relief. He understood what was happening. The preacher must have gotten his information from the news and written it into his own agenda—hijacked the uncertain and made it certain while presenting the only defense against annihilation: a love for God.

Why had he not seen it before? The blind worship of a being for whom destruction of Earth was not only necessary, but an act of love for human beings, *His* creation. He'd done it before with water, the preacher said, and now He was doing it again with fire—so be ready for the Lord's love, and accept Jesus Christ as your only true savior before it's too late.

Lenny rubbed his face into the carpet of the first stair. Imagined the preacher's face scanning the magazine articles with glee. They were saved. They were all saved. It was a miracle.

23.

He bounded into the living room and got close to the flames, stretched his whole body out.

The preacher had seen warnings in the media and used them as a way to peddle fear. It was obvious. Lenny read the message on his phone again, hoping for another rush of insight.

> We've just now found out from the police what's happened. You may not be able to read this, but know I love you all, and am praying for you. Be with you soon, Mom.

It was the last sentence that baffled him. Was she driving up to the rented house? How would she know where it was? Or did she mean they would be together in general?

Without the preacher and the magazines to worry about, Lenny assumed she meant the heavy snow. It must be worse in Albany. Roads closed. Salt trucks out.

He imagined a patchwork of flickering lights.

Maybe snow was part of the end? Lenny snatched up the newspaper and began to read. People in regions near the Arctic and Antarctic could burrow away from the surface of the Earth and live longest. But only by a few hours. Then the Earth's crust would sizzle to wisps of smoke. Nothing about snow in Albany.

But the *American Geographic* story said something that made Lenny stop reading, and just sit cross-legged by the fire.

It was that, before the universe, there was nothing.

Not even time.

Lenny pictured his wife upstairs. Carolin had come from a place where there had once been nothing.

But why was there not nothing now?

He thought of her body in the bed. Eyes behind still lids. Head on the pillow, chin tilted up in gentle defiance of sleep. Then Jane. A warm bundle of child and doll.

Lenny felt their lives as miraculous and small. But the smallness was more valuable to him than things he could not imagine. A universe with endless patches of hot and cold.

They were at the mercy of flesh and bone. Things he could not comprehend would never be greater than his daughter's hands, his wife's hair on the pillow at night like black rivers.

24.

Lenny held up his watch. He could hear the springs, the wheels, and the cogs that measured time—but which were really counting the cycles of Earth circling that great fire humans once believed was a God.

It was almost five now. The watch was made in Switzerland. Why had time never been worshipped? It seemed important enough, and existed without being visible. Maybe it's God of the future, Lenny wondered. The first nonhuman God. A force that moves without moving.

Carolin had bought the watch for Lenny nine years before, in Las Vegas. He could see her now at the craps table in fancy black shoes. Lenny had promised his mother never to gamble, so he watched with a plastic cup of Sprite because he had been sober six months.

Then came the lucky roll.

Carolin screamed and everyone looked at them. They looked at each other.

"We're on our honeymoon," Carolin said to all the people watching, as though trying to explain her good fortune.

Lenny hadn't thought about that trip to Las Vegas for a long time. But it was an important memory now. It was the first time he'd felt certain of another person's love.

In the afternoon Lenny had made Carolin get the three-stone diamond ring she wanted. When she asked what *he* wanted, he told her a tattoo. She got him a watch instead. Lenny kept holding it up to his ear.

On the last day, they saw the Elvis chapel.

"Let's get married again," Lenny said, then held up his watch. "We have time."

It was silly but made her laugh.

Sitting before the fire, a hot speck in the universe, Lenny could feel the happiness he would lose when his life ended. Memories bombarded him then, as though trying to find their way back into the world. Maybe that's what ghosts are, he thought, feelings so strong they get away.

25.

It was time to sleep. Lenny felt his eyes were closing. He was ready to lie down and disappear.

It would be light soon, and everything seemed clear now.

The preacher had taken things from magazines, and the message from Carolin's mother was about the snow. They would wake up tomorrow and go about their lives.

It had been an evening of near misses and Lenny felt grateful for everything he had seen and felt.

Driving up from Albany, Carolin thought they should turn back on account of the weather. But everyone was hungry, so when Lenny saw lights he pulled off, hoping the blizzard would lessen as they ate.

The diner had aluminum sides and a neon sign. Inside it was bright. There were people in groups of two or three. The waitress put them in a booth with a torn seat. At the next table, an old man and woman were feeding their grand-daughter. The girl's brother colored a dinosaur with crayons from a washed-out sour cream tub. A TV above the counter played *Wheel of Fortune*. The other patrons reminded Lenny of his people out west. The laughing and drinking beer, tattoos, and faded shop hats. There was an old man in the booth behind them. When he moved, Lenny felt the weight of his body. He was sitting by himself. Laughing at the things he saw on television.

Then Jane laughed because they thought there was a

rooster in the kitchen, but it was a squeaky door. When Jane tried to mimic the sound, a man with missing teeth turned from the counter to look at her. But not in a mean way. He just wanted to be in on the joke.

Outside the snow was piling up and drifting.

Carolin wanted something sweet to finish off. She ordered a slab of coconut pie, which Jane said had marshmallow in the frosting. The fork in Jane's hand looked big.

Years ago, Carolin and Lenny fed her with a plastic spoon that changed color if the food was too hot. Jane used to open her mouth when it was almost to her lips. It had amazed Lenny in the diner to think that every person who ever lived on this planet once opened their mouths to receive a little pool of something *good*.

In the background, Lenny could hear the wheel of fortune turning, and people shouting, trying to speed it up or slow it down.

An hour or so after leaving the diner they had a close call. The meal had put Carolin right to sleep and Jane was almost asleep.

On a dark road thirty miles north of where they had stopped to eat, the back end of the truck kept trying to slide. Lenny cursed himself for not loading blocks or sandbags over the wheel wells.

It was hard to see because the headlights were frosted over. Then suddenly a bright light in the distance. At first Lenny thought it was a helicopter or some mountain light on a tower. It was just so high up.

But then it was closer and brighter, almost blinding.

Lenny couldn't understand it. Carolin was still sleeping and Jane was asleep too. The light was coming right toward them as if wanting to swallow them whole. Lenny gripped the steering wheel hard but didn't know which way to turn it. The light was everywhere and everything.

The next moment they were at the side of the road. Nothing moved but the tiny skeletons of snow breaking on the windshield. The light was gone. And there was no sound, except a faint ticking from the engine.

Lenny could feel his heart high up in his body making sharp, quick beats. Carolin was still sleeping, but Jane's eyes were open.

Dad, she said, *my daddy.*

That reminded him of when she was a baby. When she was helpless and he held her like a prize.

26.

Before going upstairs to bed, there was one more thing Lenny wanted to do. So he put all his clothes on and went to the front door, for his coat and boots. Sometimes in Albany, he liked to go outside and look at their pink house, his wife and daughter inside, sleeping, eating, or watching television.

It made him feel like a ghost. Filled him with peace to know that while they *thought* they were alone—he was watching, following shadows on the wall or catching the tail of their laughter.

He walked to the far end of the property, into darkness where the road was. He stopped and looked back at the house. There was moonlight on the snow, and the trees cast moving shadows.

Suddenly, a perfect square of bright yellow.

Lenny stopped breathing. Someone was in the bathroom.

Then with a pinprick of sound, it was gone . . .

. . . the idea that happiness, more than happiness, a whole life could be measured by the turning on of a light.

It was the perfect embodiment of all that is *good*.

27.

Soon the black would drain slowly away.

He knew that, and wanted to go upstairs. Be with them. But for some time, Lenny had known that he could not go there—could not be with them in that way.

It was snowing then.

Flakes tumbled from the sky and broke apart. Lenny closed his eyes and lay down on the ice that covered the road. The truck was stiff because the engine had been off since dark. He was not far from the truck, lying on the ice, but he could not touch it. Could not touch anything.

It didn't matter anymore if the world was ending.

He had found two people where there had once been nothing.

So much of his life had been *good*.

That there was good in the world for everybody made him feel that God was just *good* and did not have a face, or a body, or a will, with rules and punishment.

God was laughter. God was sliding on ice. God was a flat tire. A blue tarp. A lake in summer. Destiny glimpsed through coincidence. The certainty of nothing.

28.

For many hours the surgeons couldn't figure out why the man on the operating table was not dying. Hard to believe with the state he was found in. Head-on collision with a state salt truck on Mountain Road.

Paramedics discovered the body in a halo of red snow. But somehow the heart had kept on. There was a woman inside the vehicle, unconscious and pinned under the engine.

The third victim, a child, was sniffed out by a rescue dog fifty yards from the crash, where she lay facedown with broken femurs and a shattered pelvis.

One of the volunteer firefighters found a doll in the wreckage. It had a dress and ice skates. He took it back to the station and washed it carefully in a sink.

After what they'd seen, the other men were not ready to go home either. So they changed clothes and drove to the hospital in their trucks.

Some of the men believed in God, and some of them didn't. The girl was in surgery, so they waited outside, taking turns to hold the doll.

The Saddest Case
of True Love

Last week I received a postcard from Italy. At first I thought it was a mistake. The message was short but very personal. The sender's father had "died peacefully" at a care facility in Seoul. The postcard was signed in black ink with a name I didn't immediately recognize. But later on the memory came back. An evening I had spent with Soyeon several years ago in Florence. She had told me about her father then, and the things he had done.

Days passed and I forgot about it. Then one evening, I was sitting by the pool, watching a helicopter circle the canyon. My wife appeared with a tray of drinks.

"Are the girls back from school?"

"Volleyball and band," she said. "I thought we might have a cocktail before they get home."

On the tray next to the glasses was the postcard from Italy. My wife pointed at it by nodding her head. "Who is Soyeon? Someone you met in Europe?"

"One of Teddy's friends."

"From Florence? Man or woman?"

"Woman."

"Why would she want you to know her father was dead? Did you meet him when you were there?"

"No, she told me about him."

My wife made herself comfortable on a lounge chair and drank slowly. She was wearing the red platform espadrilles I had bought her in the Florence duty-free.

I had only been there for an afternoon and a night. Enough time to visit a few churches, I'd thought, get the smell of incense in my clothes, stand before a few paintings and statues, the *Annunciation* or *Birth of Venus*. Teddy, my wife's friend who resided there full-time, would be in Brooklyn meeting his new gallerist, which meant I could use his apartment.

I didn't know anything about Florence itself—but had seen some illustrations in a history book on my wife's desk. There must have been other pictures, but I only remember the executions. Stacks of flaming wood with the body of a heretic tied up on a pole. Another showed platforms constructed for some drawn-out form of public torture.

Teddy was an American painter who had purposely moved to an Italian city where modern art was not possible, and so he felt no pressure when making it. His apartment was in the center of town. He had described in an email the ancient front door with blunt spikes embedded in the wood, a small stand nearby for food and newspapers—even a Florentine barber, with brushed steel chairs and bottles of green aftershave in the window. The apartment took up the second floor in a fifteenth-century building above a Chanel boutique that was once a medieval stable. Purses and bags now hung in place of bridles.

The keys had been left with one of the girls in the shop. When I arrived in the early afternoon, there was a line of tourists waiting to go in. I talked to the guard and he asked me to wait inside the door. Soyeon was with a customer, but eventually finished her sale and came over with the key. The barrel was long and uncomplicated. A smooth, rusted brown. There was a key chain with it. A red patent leather heart. Soyeon's nails were red too. When she smiled, I noticed a few of her teeth were crooked.

She was finishing early that night and wanted to walk me up to Piazzale Michelangelo. To really experience Florence, she told me, you had to leave the city altogether. I had never enjoyed grand views or sunsets, preferring the small beauty of a leaf, or the strangeness of a puddle. But before I could think of an excuse, she had moved silently back across the carpet, toward a wall of jeweled purses, where there were people waiting. She had straight black hair and white skin with freckles around her nose. Soyeon's clothes were tight on her body. She wore black heels with a pearl on each toe.

Teddy's apartment had stone floors and the walls were cold to the touch. The ceilings were fifteen feet high. Cobwebs fringed wooden beams. Over the centuries people had died and been born within a few feet of where I was standing. The two main rooms were taken up by enormous squares of canvas on dark wood easels. The rooms smelled of linseed oil and the paintings were hung with sheets, as though signifying death in the absence of their creator.

I took a cold shower, then went outside. The markets were bustling with people. I stopped to buy tin cases of chocolate almonds for my daughters, and stood listening at the edge of tour groups. Some shops sold lace collars, and I bought three. They came flat, folded in pink tissue.

Before returning to the apartment, I picked up half a loaf of bread and some tomatoes wrapped in newspaper. The apartment was dark now with the shutters closed. It felt quiet after my long walk, and I wanted to sleep again. I removed my shoes and socks and let my feet cool on the stone tiles. Then I went into the kitchen and ran cold water from the faucet into my cupped hands. After a few mouthfuls, I ate the bread and tomatoes with some black pepper on the patio. The furniture out there was plastic and faded. A few of the chairs were on their backs. One had a broken leg. I imagined drunken laughter as bodies sprawled. There were a few empty bottles, and ashtrays with floating cigarette ends.

After the food and cold water I was content to sit and read. But then I remembered Soyeon, so I brushed my teeth quickly and went outside. The shop was closed but the lights were still on. Soyeon was waiting by the door. She had changed into other clothes and was wearing plain, flat shoes. She had pulled her hair back into a ponytail and would have looked like a student, if not for a silk Chanel scarf tied around her neck.

When we started walking, my legs felt tired and I wanted to give up and find a restaurant. It was going to be a long march in the evening heat with a steep climb. But I felt powerless to stop what was now happening, as though it would have taken more energy not to go along with Soyeon's plan.

After crossing the Arno River, she began to ask questions. How did I meet my wife. How old were my two daughters. Did I have any pets. I answered in a friendly way, but was too tired to give details.

Then *she* started talking. First about the shop. Working for Chanel. Her boss from Rome. Dressing the mannequins. A Christmas card every year from Karl Lagerfeld. Then she told me about her mother and growing up in Korea. The crowd on the street had thinned by this time, and we could stroll side by side, like people who had known each other for a long time and had real things to say.

She came from a suburb of Seoul, a place I couldn't imagine. Their home was a two-room apartment that overlooked a main highway. The kitchen was full of plants. Some of the plants grew leaves you could eat. She told me there were tower blocks all around, and Laundromats—and that from her window you could see the edge of a golf course.

Her mother was eighteen when Soyeon was conceived. She was a small woman who cleaned offices, and in the evening watched soap operas on the couch with her feet tucked neatly under her body. Orphaned through war when she was three, her heart had long searched for a place to drop anchor.

Soyeon's father was much older. A businessman. A golfer. He often worked late and wore a gray suit with thin white stripes. Out of all the people in the office building, hundreds of workers, he had chosen her, Soyeon's mother.

At first it was just looks. Then a few words of greeting. After that, he unscrewed her cleaning bottles to put flowers in. Left notes with the opposite weather forecast to make her laugh. She saved his cubicle for last, making him work even later if he wanted to see her. Emptying his trash can of papers and tea cans was something Soyeon's mother looked forward to. She was young then, and wanted to keep everything her businessman had ever touched.

If no one was around, his hand sometimes touched hers. She felt her body waking from a long, impenetrable slumber. This romance went on privately for a good while because the businessman lived outside Seoul in a house with his wife, teenage daughters, and a gray kitten.

Soyeon's mother knew from soap operas that happiness often comes at a price; that once lives are tangled up, they can never be untangled. Pain is proof of something worthwhile.

Then one day he appeared at her door. It was dark out. His tie had been loosened. She wanted him to come inside.

When it was over they held hands, listening to voices from the television. The blinds were open and they could see all the lights of the city.

By the time Soyeon was born, her mother had left the

office complex and was cleaning in a small factory. There was more dirt, but also more money. She missed seeing her businessman, but other workers had realized there was something going on.

He was not there for Soyeon's actual birth, but paid for a new apartment in the same building. It was another very small home. Only big enough for two. But at night they could hear each other being tossed around by dreams.

Soyeon met her father for the first time when she was three. He came to their house and ate noodles with imitation crab. After, he sat on the couch and looked at Soyeon. He asked questions but all she wanted was to play. She attended kindergarten then, in a tower block near the factory where her mother was employed.

Soyeon remembers how much she liked her father. But their laughter led only to the sadness of being apart.

One day, they all went to the zoo. Soyeon ran from cage to cage. Her parents walked behind holding hands. Soyeon thought it was the beginning of something, but it was the end.

A week later, her mother came to get her from school with a bruise on her face. Her lip had swollen so it was easier to nod when the teachers asked if she was okay. Soyeon rubbed her mother's feet. Brought her green tea. Watered the plants and wiped the windows. Soyeon's father did not visit for many months. During this time her mother sometimes put on perfume and slipped away when Soyeon was in bed. Later there would be talking and muffled laughter. A man's voice, but not her father's.

During the winter it happened again. He was waiting for

her in a parking lot, his body shaking with jealousy and rage. Soyeon's mother told everyone she slipped on ice. A cracked rib kept her awake. Shallowed her breathing. One eye seemed like it might never open again.

The boss of the factory called her into his office. He gave her coffee from a machine. It was just plain coffee in those days that came through a nozzle into a brown cup. His hair was already gray and the staff called him "grandfather" behind his back. The boss listened to her story, then went into another room to call his wife. She told him to let the girl and her daughter live at the factory for a week. Maybe the abuser would think they had run away and give up trying to find them.

Above the factory floor was an elevated glass office where the boss liked to watch operations and entertain visitors. The lights were always on, and you reached it by metal staircase. At the very back of the factory was a row of big rooms. Some of the rooms had purple carpet and filing cabinets, while others contained enormous cupboards with spare toilet paper and cleaning supplies. The biggest room had beds and a shower. It was for technicians who came from China to fix the machines. Sometimes it took many days if a part was ordered. The technicians weren't supposed to smoke in the room. They joked with the factory staff, and showed pictures of their families.

Soyeon's mother was given the day off and told to return in the evening with a bag of things they would need to stay. An elaborate plan of coming and going was worked out so the other workers wouldn't know she was sleeping in the apartment for Chinese technicians. Each day, she would take Soyeon to day care early, then sit in the park until it was safe to arrive at work at the normal time.

In the evening, she would collect her daughter, then, after a walk and something to eat, would return to the factory after eight. Soyeon remembered the wooden sign outside day care with children's faces drawn on it. She had thought one of the faces was hers. But it was everybody and at the same time not a single person.

As we neared the top of Piazzale Michelangelo, sunlight filled the streets like gold fabric.

The part Soyeon said she remembered most was being allowed to ride her tricycle up and down the factory floor. It was quiet with the machines down. She felt good there. She remembers the smoothness of the floor. How easy it was to build up speed. The smell of cardboard and oil in one corridor. Hot plastic in another. The factory made toys. It was really a dream come true, Soyeon told me, except the room they slept in smelled like cigarettes.

Near the small cafeteria with its chilled cabinets of salad and cans of green tea, there was an unlocked room where all the broken toys went. Soyeon wanted to explore that room more than anything, and although her mother had forbidden it—after a week in the factory she got her chance, because Soyeon's father had found out where they were.

It was the middle of the night, but he was outside screaming and rattling the doors of the main entrance.

Soyeon's mother jumped out of bed and ran with her daughter to the room of defective toys. The toys were in giant boxes. They would bury themselves in broken dolls until he went away. Soyeon was lifted into one. Then her mother got in. The smell of plastic was very strong. Soyeon wanted to play but was supposed to keep her hands still.

After a while their heads popped out and they listened. Soyeon said she remembered it now like a scary cartoon. The shouting had stopped. No more rattling of the doors. Just to be certain, they stayed a bit longer, went through the toys one by one to pass the time, inspecting each doll, trying to figure out what had gone wrong and why they were in there.

When it got late they found the cafeteria and shared green tea mousse. Soyeon's mother stacked coins in place of the container. The food made them cheerful, so they walked around the factory holding hands, and singing songs they knew from television. Then suddenly he was standing in front of them. His gray suit was ripped and his shirttail hung out like a white tongue. He rushed forward and grabbed Soyeon's mother's wrists.

"Go to the toy room!" she screamed to her daughter.

But Soyeon hid behind a machine, watching as her mother broke free, then ran up the metal staircase to the raised office. Soyeon's father chased after her, as though it were a game they were playing, as though everything that was happening had been decided upon long before.

Once inside the glass room, Soyeon's mother locked the door, while her father said her name over and over. Then he stopped speaking and pulled savagely on the handle. Then he tried kicking the door but it wouldn't open. Soyeon's mother was like a fish in a bowl. Then he pounded on the door and both his hands went through as the glass shattered. As he unlocked it from inside, Soyeon's mother ran backward into a corner, raising her arms to protect herself. But instead of hitting her, the businessman went calmly to an office chair and sat down before a computer, as though he were at work.

Without knowing why, Soyeon said she left her hiding place and went up the metal stairs to the glass office. She knew there was an orange metal box with a red cross on it. She had seen it before. They had the same one at her school. It was full of medicine and white ribbon. When Soyeon got to the top of the stairs, the office was very bright, and there was glass on the floor.

Her mother was slumped over, sobbing. Then she saw her daughter standing there. "Go play," she said weakly.

Sitting in the office chair bleeding was Soyeon's father. The man who'd held her mother's hand at the zoo. Who had fed Soyeon imitation crab as she played on the carpet. There was also blood on his cheeks and on the white collar of his shirt. But mostly it dripped to the floor and onto his black shoes.

Soyeon got the orange box and took the lid off. She did not feel afraid. She took out two rolls of bandage and went to her father. She could see his eyes clearly. The expression in them made her feel good. Soyeon took the bandage and went round and round. Her only concern was to get it straight. She had wrapped dolls before, but this man was not a doll. At first the blood came through in dots like eyes watching. Then the bandage stayed white. Soyeon's mother stood up and was looking. Her father could not use his hands for anything, so kept them in the air like he was surprised at everything that had happened in the toy factory.

By this point Soyeon and I had reached the summit, a tiny square bustling with tourists and souvenir stands. The sun had almost completely sunk. It was no longer shimmering in the river, nor golden in the streets.

Soyeon said she never saw her father again after that night. But nineteen years later her mother called her apartment in Florence to say he had collapsed at his workplace. The cleaning lady found him lying on the carpet by his desk. He was alive, but unable to talk or move one side of his body.

Over the next several years, Soyeon's mother visited him at the rehabilitation hospital. She had not seen her businessman for almost two decades, but admitted there had been letters exchanged.

At first she went to the hospital once every two weeks. Then once per week, then twice. She read romance books to him aloud. Touched his hands and rubbed his arms, trying to arouse feeling in the parts of his body where there was nothing. She told him stories about their daughter in Europe, and showed pictures of her growing up. His other family didn't visit much. But if she was caught, Soyeon's mother planned to say she was his best school friend's younger sister.

Soyeon said she was sure her mother would meet the other family one day, but it never happened.

After visiting, she got home in time for her soap operas. So much had taken place since she'd begun following each show—so many ruined lives redeemed.

Sometimes she took all the postcards her daughter had sent from Italy and laid them out on the table beside his hospital bed. The nurses said he could see and he could hear. Soyeon's mother had even sent her a photograph of them together at the hospital. It was in a frame beside her bed where she could look at it.

On the steps down, Soyeon took my arm for balance and asked if it wasn't the saddest case of true love I had ever heard?

That was how she saw it.

When we got back to town, the streets were packed with tourists strolling after dinner. Some parents had let their children run ahead to the souvenir shops. The cafés were full of people talking and drinking from tiny cups.

Soyeon didn't live in the center of Florence and had to take a bus home. I waited with her at the stop. When we saw lights, she asked if I would like to see where she lived.

On my long walk back to Teddy's apartment, I imagined her face at the bus window. The silence when she got home.

She would put her bag down, pull off her shoes, and go soundlessly through the place where she lived, completely alone, but all around—the voices and faces of memory, hovering like unquenched fires.

I pictured us together on the steps at dusk.

The feeling when she touched my arm.

The moon about to rise.

The wrapping of her father's hands in white ribbon.

In the morning I locked the keys inside the apartment as I was instructed. Then I went to the Museo Ferragamo on Piazza Santa Trinità. There were paintings from his home, and photographs of Salvatore as a young designer. One wall was a display of wooden shoe lasts, with names written on the wood: Audrey Hepburn, Ingrid Bergman, the Duchess of Windsor . . .

In a dark corner at the back of the museum was a projection of some classic Hollywood film. Young women in sequined dresses and red lipstick. One of the actors was Marilyn Monroe. She had white hair and perfect eyebrows.

Soyeon had said her mother was as beautiful as a teenage girl.

That was why her father had fallen for her.

That was how she had caught the attention of such an important businessman in the office building where she cleaned.

My wife picked up the postcard and read aloud the part Soyeon had written about her father dying peacefully, at the care facility in Korea. I hadn't thought so before, but now we both agreed, it was the saddest case of true love we had ever heard.

The Doorman

S ophie is in the front row of a downtown jazz club.
It's almost three in the morning, but she wears sunglasses to hide the fact that she is blind. For a few moments,
an old man near the stage imagines she is here to meet a
younger version of himself.

When the musicians stop playing and people stand to
applaud, Sophie rises in a cloud of cigarette smoke and walks
so slowly people think she is drunk. There is no hope she will
find the steps and so tilts her body onto the stage using
elbows and knees.

The musicians have melted into the crowd. The only
sound comes from smoky bursts of laughter, shuffling feet as
people leave their seats for the bar.

Sophie is onstage trying to find the piano without knock-
ing over a microphone stand. Her hands move from side to
side, as though she is conducting. She brushes the edge of a
double bass, the pebbled roof of an amplifier. Then a stool leg
connects with the leather curve of her ballet flat. People are
looking now, curious, but also waiting for someone to bring her
down from the stage.

It's an old piano. Sophie can tell from the way it smells. The tone will be dry because the hammers are worn. She is too nervous to adjust the seat, and sizes the keyboard by spreading her fingers. The notes are steps that must be taken in a precise order. When she starts, it's soft, unexpected. People listen.

Then a face appears at the corner of the stage. The quartet leader. He has heard this song before. He knows the pressure of these fingers. The other musicians approach, but he puts out his arm to stop them. Nothing moves now but the hands of this lone pianist and the stirring of smoke over tables and chairs. Her blond hair is pinned up to reveal a neck as white as the keys.

Ray Wong steps out onstage, leans into the mic.

"I remember you," he says.

The blind girl bites her lip. Blinks under her sunglasses. The audience thinks it's funny. Ray Wong lifts his trumpet from the stand. The people watching believe it's part of the show.

The other musicians stand there. Poised for a signal to come onstage. But the trumpet player holds them back with a stare, then raises the instrument to his lips.

The bartenders watch with their hands buried in ice. Nothing like this has ever happened, not with someone from the audience—a woman people thought was drunk.

The man with the trumpet is a jazz legend. His concerts in Japan and Germany sell out months in advance. People say he can control your emotion with his breath. They say he learned music before words—that he never left Chinatown until he was twenty—that he lived above an illegal pet shop in an alley and played for the animals—that his first trumpet was found in the trash.

The truth is that Ray Wong was born in a hot room above a Laundromat off Canal Street. It was October 15, 1981. His mother didn't think she could push him out all the way. The pain was so great she convinced herself they would both die. After, she lay and couldn't speak. Empty but full. Her shaking body drenched with sweat.

Ray's father carried their son to the window in search of a breeze. He raised the blinds and described to his newborn son how there were people outside in sunglasses. Cars parked up and down both sides of the street. Tables in the vegetable market, heaped with leafy bundles and basins of turtles and frogs.

"One day," he told his son, "we will go there together and choose things to eat."

Their apartment consisted of two rooms. One for cooking and one for sleeping. Ray's parents worked in a kitchen at Wo Lee's Late-Night Restaurant.

The Laundromat below their apartment was owned by Mrs. Fang. She watched baby Ray in the afternoons when his parents left for work. She put him in a basket of towels where he could see clothes turning in the machines. When he was able to crawl, Ray liked to slap his hands against the warm glass doors. The Laundromat smelled of soap in the morning and fish soup at night. It was always bright, with people in canvas shoes folding things from the dryers. The floor was a grid of black and yellow tiles, and there was a folding table for mah-jongg.

After shutting down the machines, sweeping up, and lowering a grate over the front window of the shop, Mrs. Fang carried Ray upstairs and fed him dinner. When she sang songs, Ray pulled at his diaper. When she set him in his crib, he touched his feet in the darkness and listened for the knock of her broom in corners.

On warm nights, Ray lay with his eyes open, feeling things he could not articulate. Then the hushed chatter of his parents coming. The smell of food and smoke in their clothes.

On the street below, opposite the Laundromat was a bar where musicians often met after concerts to drink and play the pieces only musicians like to hear.

In August, when it was hot, they would sit on the steps to smoke. Sometimes they brought their instruments outside. The Chinese American baby in the upstairs apartment, listening through an open window, would never meet a single one of these men or women, never learn their names, never see their faces, nor follow their hands prancing over strings and keys. Yet into his small body went all they gave. All they had seen and done. All they had once wished for.

When Sophie was born four miles north on January 14, 1987, her parents didn't know what to do about her blindness. They saw many doctors who said different things. For her, childhood was the sensation of sound, the anticipation of hands, the joy of foods she liked in her mouth. The pain and humiliation of having her teeth brushed.

After school, Sophie would sit with her nanny in Central Park beside the lake, listening to the footsteps of children chasing toy boats. She knew everything had a shape, a temperature, and a feeling—but color was something unimaginable. Sometimes she was taken onto a meadow for something to eat.

To the delight of her parents, Sophie was liked at school. People helped her in the lunchroom—carried her tray and read the names of foods. She was allowed to sit out of certain sports but got to wear a gym uniform anyway. But she was never invited to birthdays at the puppet theater in Central Park, nor on weekend trips to the Hamptons. In high school, she had tried to organize slumber parties, but other girls were always so busy.

Sophie's best friends were her parents. They watched television together in the evenings, filling in details over the silence of an onscreen kiss. But so much of what was happening Sophie could tell from the music.

One summer she went to Paris for three weeks. Her parents bought her a dress of dotted swiss from a boutique on Avenue Montaigne. She had dreamed of meeting a boy in France. Wearing the dress and being touched in it.

When Sophie was fifteen, her father was cutting an apple and the knife slipped. There must have been blood, because she found him sitting on the floor with paper towels on his hand.

When the paramedics came, Sophie stood listening to the unfamiliar sounds of Velcro and plastic seals being ripped. Then she stood on Fifth Avenue with Stan the doorman as the ambulance doors closed and her father was taken away.

Stan had been head doorman since 1983. He took a bus from Harlem each morning, and a bus home each night when his shift was over.

Stan found Sophie a chair in his office and made her some coffee. There was music on the radio, and she asked Stan what it was. He turned up the volume.

"You ain't never heard jazz before, Miss Wilkins?"

"I've never had coffee before either," she said.

The name of the song on the radio was "Stairway to the Stars." When the music ended, Stan said that it had been recorded in Paris on May 23, 1963. Then the radio announcer said the very same thing. Stan ordered a pizza, which they ate together waiting for Sophie's mother to come home.

A week later, Sophie was getting into the elevator with her nanny when Stan caught the doors and handed her a compact disc.

"Here's something," he said. "It's not coffee but still good."

Two weeks after that, she was getting out of a taxi with her parents, when Stan opened the door asked what she thought of the music.

"What music?" her father said.

Stan half expected the girl to have lost the disc. Put it down somewhere and forgotten. But Sophie went toward him and reached out her arms in a way that meant she wanted to hug.

"If I keep playing it," Sophie admitted, "I'm going to break the machine."

"Oh, it's meant to be played," Stan told her. "And loud too."

On the bus home that night, Stan realized how fond he had grown of the blind girl. How much he liked doing things for her.

When Ray Wong was a teenager, he spent most of his free time in thrift stores, searching for vinyl nobody else thought was important. His family had moved to a bigger apartment in Queens when he was five. On Sundays, his parents took him to a park in Flushing. His mother spread a blanket on the grass and they ate dumplings from plastic bowls. Old people sang and played games. Ray used to take off his shoes and chase birds.

Mr. and Mrs. Wong forced him to work hard at school, and hoped he might be the first Wong to attend university. They bought a cheap car for trips to the beach with Mrs. Fang—who was now old and lived with them.

By the time Ray was a teenager, he had saved up enough money to buy the trumpet he wanted, a 1964 Olds Special.

He had learned to read music at seven, and taught himself to play piano on the old upright at the Chinese-American Community Center. His teachers handed him scores by Mozart and Schubert. Tried to involve him in concerts and orchestras, but to Ray this was music that belonged inside a jewelry box.

People rarely saw him without headphones on. Several times he was almost hit crossing streets in Flushing. He lived for jazz. It was all he cared about. And so at fourteen, his parents allowed their son to take the subway to Harlem twice a week for trumpet lessons with Kiss Me Williams— whose records could be found in almost every secondhand shop in New York City.

Mr. and Mrs. Wong were happy their son had a hobby, and hoped he might one day put down his trumpet and pick up some chemistry books. But by the end of high school, Ray Wong was already known in most of the underground jazz clubs as "the Pearl" or "Mr. Noodle," on account of his frantic runs.

A few of the old-timers said they could hear the influence of Kiss Me Williams. They wondered what ever became of him, whether he was living or dead.

It was only a matter of time before Sophie asked her parents for a piano. A few days after it arrived Stan saw her in the lobby.

"I heard somebody in this building—I won't say who— got something big and noisy."

It took months to find the right teacher. Eventually, her father called Juilliard, and a slim Jewish girl with dyed black hair appeared one day at the apartment door.

"Tell me what you love," she said. "And I'll teach you how to play it."

It took Ray Wong years to find his voice on the trumpet. He practiced many hours a day, and never missed a lesson. Kiss Me Williams had not only taught him how to play his instrument—but also, how to talk the language of producers, booking agents, and the session musicians he would come to depend on for income.

Ray's parents sometimes went to jazz clubs and listened over glasses of hot water. They liked to see people nod appreciatively when he played difficult parts. Their favorite song was "Afternoons with Mrs. Fang," which Ray wrote a few months after she died. It was the first piece on an album he was writing called *The Wong Way*.

Ray's teacher recorded his first song in Louisville, Kentucky, at the beginning of 1947. He wore a double-breasted, pin-striped suit. It still hung in his closet but was full of small holes. Soon after, he went to St. Louis. Then New York City.

When the lesson was over, Ray sometimes used the bathroom before the long subway ride to Flushing. On the wall was a black-and-white photograph of his teacher with a woman. Once Ray asked if that woman was his wife. The old man laughed. "That's Marilyn Monroe."

"How come you have a picture of her in your bathroom?"

"Because when she sang 'Happy Birthday' to the president of the United States—it just so happens that yours truly was on the horn, with Hank Jones on piano."

Sometimes Ray brought his teacher salt-and-pepper

shrimp, or hot and sour soup with extra croutons. The young student was curious about the old man's life, but their lesson never went beyond that old suit in the closet, or the black-and-white picture on the bathroom wall.

As Ray earned money from his gigs, he wanted to take more lessons and come to Harlem every day. But his teacher had another job, and sometimes left early in the morning.

One spring, someone hand-delivered a letter to Ray's home in Queens. It was an offer for two records and a European tour. Ray read it again on the train to Harlem and tried to imagine his teacher's face.

But when he showed it, the old man gave it back to him and said his eyes were bad—told Ray just to read it aloud. He listened to what the letter said, then went into his bedroom. A moment later he appeared with a battered instrument case.

"You could probably get a new one with your own name on the side, but use mine until that's figured out."

Ray took the case from his teacher and brushed the dust off.

"I didn't know your name was Stan?"

His teacher walked him to the subway and said good-bye at the top of the steps. "Go show 'em how we do it in Harlem, boy—and don't let them call you Mr. Noodle no more."

By the time he was twenty-three, Ray Wong had played with Wynton Marsalis at Lincoln Center, and his second album was a bestseller in fourteen countries including Japan, Germany, and Sweden. One night, midway through a concert at Carnegie Hall, Ray listened to a voice mail during inter-mission. It was from a building manager on Fifth Avenue. A staff member had died while on duty. Ray's name and phone number had been entered in the employee records as "next of kin."

The building manager wanted Ray to see the body and pick up the old man's things. There was a horn player from Lagos in the audience with his wife, and before the next set began, Ray asked if he would continue the concert in his absence.

As the taxi cut through Central Park, Ray realized it had been almost a year since he'd seen his old teacher. When the taxi pulled up, there were two police cars, and the building manager had forms for Ray to sign. The body had already gone to the morgue, if Ray wanted to see it. The building manager was confused as to how they knew each other. He couldn't believe it when Ray told him about the lessons, the moth-eaten suit, the old records with Stan's face on them, and playing horn for the president and Marilyn Monroe on the White House lawn. The building manager had thought Stan was just another old man.

When the police left, the manager went inside. It was quiet as though nothing had happened. Ray looked up past the white-trimmed purple awning, up the cement walls of the building. Most lights were off, but from an open window three floors up, he could hear the tinkling of a piano.

Someone was playing jazz. He listened and, with each break in the traffic, could hear hands that were slow but sure on the keys. Ray put his trumpet case down and sat on a low wall. Central Park was dark now, the footpaths long and empty. He wondered if it was a pianist he knew, someone he had played with.

Mrs. Fang once told him that after death, spirits sometimes hang around, watching the people they loved.

So Ray took out his trumpet and played along to the few, faint bars of music that drifted down to the street. One or two lights flicked on. The building manager appeared with a lit cigarette.

When the piano stopped, Ray lowered his trumpet, then packed it away in Stan's old case. By the time Sophie had dressed and come downstairs, Ray was gone and the building manager was back in his small room watching baseball.

Sophie's parents thought their daughter was trying to express grief when she explained what she wanted the next morning. But a week later she asked again, and convinced them it was something she had to do. Her father was dead against it.

"At least let me go in with you," he implored her.

But his daughter was determined.

"Well, you just can't go alone, Sophie, it's unthinkable."

Sophie's mother put down her coffee cup purposefully. "She'll be in college next year, Martin. She'll be alone then."

Sophie's father seemed wounded. "You're supposed to be on my side."

Remembering a line from her favorite film, Sophie smiled. "There are no sides, Dad."

And so the following weekend, Sophie's parents drove her around to the different jazz clubs in their black Mercedes, watching as she disappeared inside after chatting with the doormen. They figured she would give up after one night, but three weekends later they were still dodging drunks and crawling through industrial streets in Bushwick and Long Island City—on the hunt for open doors with people outside holding cigarettes and glasses.

Live jazz was nothing like recorded jazz, and Sophie lingered in each place longer than she had to. Men offered to buy her drinks then laughed when she told them she was blind and seventeen.

Then at 2:48 A.M. on a Sunday morning, she descended the carpeted stairs of a small club in NoHo and heard him playing a trumpet version of "Stairway to the Stars." There was a piano, and all she had to do was get up onstage during intermission, and start to play.

Stan had gone to work that morning with a sense something might happen. He'd been up most of the night with pains in his chest. And his legs were going numb. It was hard to dress and walk to the bus stop.

On the journey south, he passed a group of children going to school. Boys and girls in uniforms. One of the boys had thin ankles and long feet. He was holding a folder and walking quickly, trying to keep up with the older children. For some reason, the boy looked up when the bus went by, and caught a face staring at him through the glass.

Stan remembered then how it felt when he was young. His house had a porch and stood at the end of a dirt track.

He used to watch his mother load the stove with wood. He remembered her voice like no time had passed, not words exactly, but the tone of how she spoke, like ripples through his body.

There were many things he would like to have told her. He wondered if they would meet again. If she would recognize him as her son, or is memory something we don't get to keep, that gets left behind in the world, to live again as music.